MW01241696

BRAVING THE WESTERN WINDS

Braving the Western Winds

Nikhil Chandavarkar

Marmontina Books

Braving the Winds —1st. ed.

ISBN: 9798544024460

Imprint: Independently published

For all those committed to braving the western winds

CONTENTS

	Prologue	11
1	Stolbetsin survives	14
2	The Cabal	17
3	Reforming Roxolana	25
4	The Peace Pilgrims	28
5	Brewing up a War	37
6	Saraybas	48
7	Time for War	62
8	A Simmering Stew	73
9	Uralin and Taraski	78
10	October 1917	86
11	A National Home	91
12	The Peace Treaty	101
13	Better Days Ahead	112
14	Piastya	119
15	Feeding the War Beast	122
16	The Free City of Gutanya	124
17	Neutrality	133
18	Endgame	140
	Epilogue	149

PROLOGUE

Khoryviev Opera House
Khoryviev, Roxolana
1 September 1911

The emperor appeared in the royal box at the Khoryviev Opera House. The audience grew silent and rose to face him. Next to him were his oldest daughters, the Grand Duchesses Oksana and Svetlana, and Prince Bogdan, the heir to the throne of the neighboring kingdom of Bilguria. The audience then broke in unison into the hymn "God, Save the Tsar." They repeated the anthem three times and finished with cries of "hurrah." The emperor nodded in acknowledgment and sat down.

The theatre was packed. The Tsar's visit to the city of Khoryviev in Western Roxolana was long-anticipated and tickets to this show were limited and restricted to local notables, visiting nobility, and select officials. In the front row, just below the royal box sat the head of the armed forces, the palace commandant, the finance minister, and the prime minister and interior minister, Pavel Arsenievich Stolbetsin.

▲ ▲ ▲

At the second intermission, just before midnight, the finance minister, Vitaly Nikandrovich Korolyov, took leave of the prime minister.

"Pavel Arsenievich, I must say goodbye as I have to leave for the capital."

"Ah, how I wish I could leave with you!" replied Stolbetsin with characteristic candor. Stolbetsin never hesitated to speak his mind, rarely caring about political correctness. Surrounded by a sea of sycophants, His Majesty, in particular, valued Stolbetsin's frankness, even if at times it tried his patience. "These royal trips with their long list of events are so tedious; I long to be back with my family. My wife worries, what with nineteen attempts on my life to date."

"But you are safe, here, Pavel Arsenievich. I hear your head of police, General Kurortov, has placed ninety-two gendarmes here in the theater, led by fifteen officers. The place is crawling with them." The finance minister gestured with his chin up to the royal box, which was now empty. The emperor and his companions had left to mingle with the notables awaiting his Majesty outside the box. "Above all, His Majesty is safe."

"See you back in the capital, then, Viktor Nikandrovich, *do svidenya!*"

Stolbetsin watched the finance minister leave. Then, he turned around to the half-empty hall. Some two meters away stood a short clean-shaven young man, with beady narrow-set eyes peering through wire-rim glasses, a hooked nose, and pale skin, underdressed to this black-tie event, looking curiously out of place, and clutching a playbill as if he had never been to such a performance before. Clearly from his appearance a Mazar, the boy looked like a petty office worker. How on earth had he obtained a ticket to this exclusive event?

Their eyes met and they looked at each other silently. The young man surprisingly did not avert his gaze as someone in his lower station would normally have done in the presence of the prime minister of his country.

All of a sudden, the young man drew from his pocket a Browning pistol and fired two shots. Stolbetsin did not flinch or duck for cover but continued to look him straight in the eyes.

The first shot hit the decoration on the prime minister's chest: the cross of the Order of St. Vladimir and was deflected down, prevented from entering his body by the bullet-proof vest he had taken to wearing under his shirt ever since the first attempt on his life years ago. But the second bullet pierced his hand, went through the wall of the orchestra pit, and hit the concertmaster in the leg. The concertmaster cried out, but Stolbetsin remained silent despite the pain in his hand.

Stolbetsin stayed in the moment. The young man ran to the exit but was stopped by several patrons, who grabbed him roughly.

"Lynch the anarchist!" cried one of the patrons. "Throttle him! String him up!" yelled another, holding the man with his arms behind his back, so the first could punch him in the belly. A fourth patron punched the young man in the face, "Dirty anarchist!" A fifth kicked him in the shins. "Break his limbs! Take out his eyes!" The young man squealed in pain as a sixth ripped off his glasses and stomped on them. "Who let this filthy creature in?" cried a seventh. Another blow from a patron took out the assailant's two front teeth. The man squealed, falling to the floor. Others began to stomp on him and kick his sides. The gendarmes hurried up in a vain attempt to save the youth from his tormentors.

As the men beat up the assailant, five doctors present in the parterre arrived to succor the prime minister. They identified themselves to the gendarmes as Professors Rein, Chernov, Obolensky, Makovsky, Surgeon Galin, and Dr. Afanasyev.

Dr. Afanasyev tore off a piece of Stolbetsin's shirtsleeve and made a makeshift tourniquet to stop the bleeding from his hand. Meanwhile, the Tsar, hearing the commotion, had returned to the royal box with his party.

Many in the audience began to sing the national anthem out of solidarity with their prime minister. Others recited the Orthodox Yeshuan prayer "Save, O Lord, Thy People." The entire cast of Rimsky-Korsakov's opera *The Tale of Tsar Saltan* came out on stage to sing along.

Stolbetsin made the sign of the cross to the royal family. With the prime minister's bleeding stopped, orderlies carried him out on a stretcher to the waiting ambulance. In the vehicle, Stolypin said, "Inform His Majesty that I am ready to die for him and my Motherland."

1. STOLBETSIN SURVIVES

Royal Hospital, Khoryviev
September 1911

"How are you feeling, Pavel Arsenievich?" asked Viktor Vladimirovich Shubin, a conservative monarchist member of parliament and friend of the prime minister who had come to the hospital to see him.

"None the worse for wear, Viktor Vladimirovich. The doctors say I will soon be ready to leave and travel home."

"You were very lucky, Pavel Arsenievich. How is your hand?"

"I will have to dictate for a while or learn to write with my left hand. But the doctors tell me that in a matter of weeks, I should have full use of my right hand again, but with the loss of some sensation. Pity I did not raise my left hand when the boy fired, but it was a reflex reaction."

"Yes, that was the second bullet that hit your hand; but the first bullet could have entered your body."

"Thank God I was wearing my Order of St. Vladimir and my bullet-proof vest. I trust that vest more than I do our damn police."

"But General Kurortov, your vice-minister, who oversees the police assured us..."

"Ignore whatever he says," interrupted Stolbetsin. "Kurortov is my vice-minister in name, only. I have kept him on only out of respect for His Majesty, as the Empress believes Kurortov has protected the royal family well. In reality, Kurortov answers to no master, except perhaps to Mammon and his demons on earth." Stolbetsin crossed himself the Orthodox way, beginning with the right breast. "Kurortov has a large unaccounted, unaudited cash budget granted him by the Tsar for undercover activities. Heaven only knows what the weasel does with all of it. And where else he takes bribes from; one can only guess."

"The interrogation of the would-be assassin, Dima Benhorov, has revealed that he was an *agent provocateur* of the police working undercover to ferret out terrorists and anarchists. He was working for Kurortov."

"Doesn't surprise me at all. Take note: soon they will kill the boy off in prison and say he committed suicide. Case closed. The living dossier was destroyed! The official story will be that this fellow was acting alone, not on behalf of his tribe or any revolutionary group, that he was a disaffected individual with no personal grudge against me, but was a die-hard solo anarchist hitting out against the State, which I personify as head of government. Am I not right? But tell me, Viktor Vladimirovich, what are the papers saying about the attempt on my life?"

"Very interesting. The leftist press says that terrorism is the result of social injustices. The rightist press says that the concessions your government has already made to progressive forces have further fueled terrorism and anarchism. The only sober assessment, which I feel is spot on, is this little editorial in the *Novoye Vremya*. I have brought a copy with me, because I feel it is the only authentic voice in this journalistic swamp, even if, as you know, the writers for this paper are no friends of yours."

"So, what do they say that is so 'authentic'?"

"The headline reads 'Stolbetsin: A Threat to the Tribe and its Conquests and the Rise of the Forces of Darkness.'"

"Sounds melodramatic – forces of darkness!" Stolbetsin crossed himself again.

"Hold on, Pavel Arsenievich, they make sense, and I think they have hit the nail on the head."

"Read it out to me, Viktor Vladimirovich — slowly so I can ponder as you read."

"The forces of darkness are on the march again…This is a challenge to the Roxolan people, a slap in the face of Roxolan parliamentarism. This is not an isolated crime but an assault on Roxolana. It was not the sufferings of the proletariat that raised the hand of this would-be murderer, the son of a millionaire, but a man's feelings for his tribe, which has begun to encounter obstacles to its conquests. Stolbetsin was planning the nationalization of credit. Stolbetsin stands for Roxolan nationalism, and for that, this son of the tribe sought to make him a martyr; but he failed."

"Indeed, surprisingly accurate, and discreet, without calling the boy a Mazar. What an unlikely would-be assassin. He looked so pale and miserable, that little Mazar standing behind me in the theater. Poor boy, maybe he indeed thought he was performing a heroic feat to defend the interests of his tribe."

"That's a charitable Yeshuan reaction on your part, Pavel Arsenievich. You are not swearing at him. I know I would be!"

"What good is faith if one does not practice it, Viktor Vladimirovich? What does our Savior say about enemies like this fellow?"

"Forgive your enemies, for they know not what they do."

"Precisely. This boy will soon be dead; take my word for it. They will kill him in jail or give him a quick show trial and hang him. But he is a mere patsy. The dark forces that the paper talks about do indeed exist."

"Don't they mean by dark forces the reactionaries here and the conservatives, who seemed so peeved by you? I have heard both groups say that someone should do away with you."

"Of course, they are all furious with me; but I'm merely doing my job. I do what is best for Roxolana. That is my duty. I don't seek to pander to them. My loyalty is to the emperor alone."

"Fair enough. But who, in your opinion, Pavel Arsenievich, are the dark forces?"

"They lie in the West, Viktor Vladimirovich. The paper was right in mentioning the tribe. Only I would have written Tribe, with an uppercase T. The winds that power the sails of small sailors like Benhorov lie in the financial districts of the Western capitals. The dark forces are the infamous Cabal. These are the financiers who deny us loans because they say we don't treat well the members of their tribe here in our country. They want to topple the Tsar and they see me as strengthening the monarchy."

"Yes, the Cabal. The hidden power behind the visible governments of the West."

"None other."

2. THE CABAL

<u>October 1911</u>

"Yes, I admit it didn't work, despite the best of efforts and all the planning that went into it," lamented the North Vespucian financier Jakob Gondol in the oak-paneled study of banker Lord Nissim Edom in Lynden, the capital of Great Pryden, where several like-minded bankers had gathered. "But we'll get him next time!" he assured them, with a glint in his eye.

Lord Edom was the unofficial godfather of the group, the wealthiest and most influential, and all the others deferred to him. He allowed them free rein to speak and intervened only at crucial moments, usually to set the tone and arrive at conclusions and decisions.

"It was, from the start, a hair-brained scheme," remarked the Gallic banker Nathan Vogel, "to use as an assassin, of all people, that silly fop and damn daddy's boy, Dima Benhorov! *Ce satané fils à papa*! Why didn't they use a proper marksman, preferably a Slav, trained to kill? Why did they have to point the finger at our tribe by choosing an assassin from among our people? What lunacy!"

"General Kurortov, who oversees the police, assured us that this scheme would work!" explained Gondol, "Benhorov, so he claimed, was an excellent double-agent of his, who had infiltrated all anarchist milieus and had free access both to officialdom and the underworld."

"Yes, well, Benhorov didn't deliver, did he?" clucked the Ostmarkian banker, Salomon Safirberg. "An amateur who couldn't shoot straight."

"It was General Kurortov who let us down," griped Gondol. "The fault is entirely his. That spendthrift, with the pompous title of Vice Minister of the Interior, who is so easily bribed, apparently doesn't know his head from his arse. Not to speak of his idiot henchmen, Colonel Stavrovitch and Lieutenant Vershinin. No good, any of them! A band of bunglers! What a waste of good bribes! Nineteen attempts organized so far on Stolbetsin's life, and all of them have failed." He repeated, raising his voice, "All of them! Not even the bomb that went off at Stolbetsin's *dacha* — it merely injured guests and two of his children, giving our anarchists and revolutionaries a worse name still!"

"I read that the first bullet at the opera house hit Stolbetsin's medal of the Order of St Vladimir," said Adrian Paucus, a financier based in Berstadt, the capital of the Theudian Empire.

"Yes," said Lord Edom, "he was protected by a Yeshuan cross, to boot! I can see what the Orthodox monarchists will say: 'saved from a Mazar assassin's bullet by a Yeshuan cross.'"

"But, to be fair to the assailant, Stolbetsin was also wearing a bullet-proof vest," explained Gondol, "or else the doctors and ballistics experts say Benhorov's first bullet, deflected down by the cross, would have entered Stolbetsin's body and lodged itself in his liver, leading to a slow and painful death. Pity, it didn't happen that way."

"That's why shooting him is no good," said Vogel, "It *has* to be a bomb."

"Or a shot to the head," suggested Lord Edom. "That would work too!"

"No worries," replied Gondol, "next time, we'll take him out properly."

"Well, we have missed him nineteen times!" lamented Safirberg.

"You realize," said Adrian Paucus, "that Stolbetsin is the biggest obstacle to our plans for Roxolana. Even more than that reluctant, incompetent Tsar."

"Yes," added Vogel, "Stolbetsin is strengthening the position of the Tsar instead of weakening it, as we want."

"Our Trojan Horse," concluded Gondol, "cannot unload its saboteurs while the battleship of state moves inexorably forward under 'Captain' Stolbetsin."

"You all know, don't you," said Nathan Vogel, "that Stolbetsin runs the show. They say the Tsar is his puppet."

"No, I don't believe that," said Gondol, "because the Tsar has to manage quite a balancing act between Stolbetsin, the reactionary nobility, the conservative constitutional democrats — the *Kadets* — and the socialists."

"Yet, Stolbetsin is strong as ever," said Lord Edom, "although both the conservative and the liberal press claim he has been weakened. It is all spin to try to undermine him. But he remains solid. True to his name, he is a column of strength."

"Funny, isn't it," said Paucus, "he remains strong, even though all sides seem to hate him."

"Well, the Tsar has his back," explained Safirberg. "Yes, there are moments when the Tsar is frustrated with him, but whenever Stolbetsin is attacked, the Tsar defends him to the hilt."

"And Stolbetsin can't be bought, like Kurortov, can he?" asked Lord Edom.

Gondol shook his head. "Rich by birth, thrifty, frugal, abstemious, faithful to his wife, he remains incorruptible. What a pity!"

"So, not even honey traps would work?" asked Vogel.

Gondol shook his head again. "Not even the prettiest girl in the world will sway him. He loves his wife, Oksana, writes to her daily, and is not known to have kept any mistresses."

"Stolbetsin is said to be better for our tribe in Roxolana than other noblemen," noted Adrian Paucus, "What do you think, Gondol?"

"He grew up," elaborated Gondol, "on a family estate in a very diverse district in Western Roxolana, where nearly a fifth of the population was Mazar, another fifth Lithuanian, and another fifth Piastyan. He began to see Roxolans as a minority there and became interested in preserving their rights. He is more sensitive to the multicultural nature of the Roxolan Empire and minority rights than any other nobleman."

"Yes, but he is *not* one of us," declared Lord Edom. "He cannot be counted on to defend *our people's* interests. Sensitivity to diversity or minority rights is not the same thing as actively protecting our tribe."

"No, it isn't," agreed Vogel.

"What is this twenty-year plan for Roxolana he has?" asked Safirberg. "He claims, 'give me twenty years of peace and you won't recognize Roxolana.'"

"It is a plan to move Roxolana into the twentieth century," explained Gondol. "It includes making peasants small landowners, giving workers some health and unemployment insurance, and expanding primary education until it becomes universal."

"That's all well and good," said Lord Edom dismissively, "but I hear he intends to implement his plan without foreign loans. And that is *not* a good thing, as we say in the *Mazarish* language. *Doss ish nit a gudesh Ding.*"

"Yes, Stolbetsin saw how nigh impossible it was for Roxolana to float loans through our banks during the 1904-5 naval war with the Kingdom of Reben," explained Gondol, "while *all* five of us were financing the Rebenese. He knows that taking our loans would make his country beholden to us, just as the Rebenese now are."

"Well, anyway, since 1904, I have forbidden our bank in Lynden to float any bond offerings for Roxolana," said Lord Edom. "That gives us economic and political leverage over the country and the possibility of advancing the interests of our tribe in Roxolana and opening up the country to our investments, which the Tsar and Stolbetsin have been resisting."

"Our bank in Lutecia has done the same," said Vogel.

"And ours, too, in New Lynden," added Gondol.

"Same at our bank in Vedunia," confirmed Safirberg.

"As well as ours in Berstadt," said Paucus.

"Good, so, none of us are breaking ranks, then," concluded Lord Edom. "Even though that means foregone profit for all of us."

"How then," asked Vogel, "will Stolbetsin finance his twenty-year plan?"

"With gold," replied Gondol. "You know Roxolana has huge gold deposits. The metal comes out of the ground slowly, with primitive mining techniques, but it does come out. Alas, the Roxolan *grivna* is backed one-hundred percent by gold."

"We have been unable," said Lord Edom, "to launch a proper debt-based currency in Roxolana because of Stolbetsin and his former finance minister, Severin Yureivich Witwer, as well as his current one, Vitaly Nikitayevich Korolyov. A die-hard nationalist, Stolbetsin is also planning to nationalize credit and banks. Can you imagine what a setback that is for international banking, not to mention for the interests of those of our tribe who lend money in Roxolana?"

"Yes, I don't like this gold-based currency, either," concurred Vogel. "How can we make money by collecting interest if there is a gold-based currency? Gold just sits there; it earns us nothing. We need to introduce urgently a debt-based currency and a central bank that *we* control, just as we have here in Pryden and Gallia, and if all goes well, soon in the Republic of North Vespucia."

"If we can topple the Tsar's government, push the country into debt," suggested Safirberg, "then that gold could be brought over here to the West for safekeeping as collateral for the loans. Then the *grivna* would be ours!"

"Yes, well, we'll have to run up Roxolana's debts through a war," reasoned Lord Edom, "by bringing the country into a conflict with Theudaland and Ostmark, exploiting the complex set of mutual defense treaties they have set up. Then, as we loan Roxolana money to buy arms, we demand the gold as surety!"

"Indeed!" concurred Paucus. "That always works."

"To help our coreligionists and remove all remaining restrictions on them," added Gondol, "we need to put people from our tribe in charge over there — with their names changed, of course, to hide their origins. We need as many members of our tribe as possible running that country and especially the secret police apparatus, the *Okhrana*, for our plans to succeed and for us to wrest control of the state and the economy."

"The bottom line, then, is this: The Tsar must go!" said Vogel. "All of us must do our part to bring that about."

"I am investing twenty million *talents* for regime change through our charitable foundations," announced Gondol, "and have offered a reward of 1.5 million *talents* just for killing the emperor. I detest that man with every fiber in my body."

"But you have never met him, Gondol!" remarked Vogel.

"I don't need to," retorted Gondol. "I just observe how he keeps our people down, how he incites *pogroms* against them. We need a revolution over there! Throw his whole court out! Kill them all, like in 1789 in Gallia!"

"Yes, well, between us, we must admit," explained Lord Edom, "that the Tsar doesn't need to 'incite' *pogroms*. Many of those *pogroms* are an expected reaction to the thankless tax collecting role on behalf of the landowners that our people have taken on over the centuries — tax farming. The Kozak horse people, in particular, seem to have it in for our tribe; they feel exploited by our tax-farmers and moneylenders. Then, there is the liquor monopoly that the nobles have granted our people. The peasants and the Orthodox Church claim that taverns owned by our tribe serve to spread alcoholism among the poor purely for our profit."

21

"All that explosive information unfavorable to us must be kept out of the press and other publications," warned Vogel. "For the world public, the *pogroms* must always appear unprovoked, the result of deep racial hatred that outsiders unleash on our people."

"Alas, we don't yet control the press in Roxolana, Vogel, as we do here in the West," replied Gondol, "so, regrettably, the narrative that our people bring *pogroms* upon themselves by provoking the peasants through tax-farming, usury, and liquor traffic, is common currency among journalists and other writers."

"All that will change," announced Lord Edom. "In time, we will control the press there too, when our people take over Roxolana. Then, history will be very kind to our tribe; for we shall write it."

"Well, we have all been funding the revolutionary movement," said Vogel, "through the branches of our charity organizations in Roxolana."

"Indeed, Vogel," concurred Safirberg. "Fortunately, despite the ethnic quotas for our people, a disproportionately large number students at the universities in Roxolana happen to be from our tribe. And they are the most vocal and rebellious. The recent protests in Khoryviev, led by the students, were orchestrated and funded through our charity organizations. Our charities finance the printing of revolutionary pamphlets, for placards, and sloganeering. We even provide the socialists and anarchists with small arms to fight back against the Kozak cavalry."

"One of the happy byproducts of Stolbetsin's development plans," explained Gondol, "is the rise in literacy. The workers and peasants can now read our pamphlets about revolution and about overthrowing the monarchy. But that is not enough. We need effective spearheads for the revolution — we need a trusted 'vanguard of the proletariat,' made up of spearheads from our tribe."

"Any candidates for such spearheads, Gondol?" asked Lord Edom. "Even though the actual proletariat is small compared to the agricultural labor."

"Well, *milord*, Paucus and I have already recruited two brilliant Roxolan intellectuals in exile, one based in Lutecia and another in Helvetia. Both are compelling orators and fanatic believers in socialism. They think clearly and write well. Both have many published pamphlets to their names, which our charities have funded. They write in a simple, direct style that the common man can understand."

"What are their names, Gondol?" asked Vogel.

"The first is Lazar Danilovich Schwarzstein, who hails from the Black Sea port city of Yulissa, and the second, who comes from the Roxolan heartland, is called Vadim Ignatovitch Urganov."

"But, can they be trusted?" inquired Lord Edom. "Are they *bona fide* members of our tribe?"

"Yes, both of them are," confirmed Paucus. "All four of Schwarzstein's grandparents are Mazars. As for Uraganov, he is one-quarter Mazar. His mother is half Mazar. Her father converted to Orthodox Yeshuanism merely for economic and social advancement. Her mother is an Orthodox Yeshuan, but her father's family name is Banke. Plus, Vadim is fully loyal to us."

"Good East European Mazar name, Banke," observed Vogel.

"Now, as Gondol said," continued Paucus, "Uraganov currently lives in Helvetia, where I go regularly on business. I serve as Urganov's sponsor and handler."

"Now, Adrian Paucus, you have chosen for yourself a nice, non-descript Western name," proposed Lord Edom, "to blend in with the outsiders."

"Yes, I have," acknowledged Paucus, whose real name was Issur Leibovich Goldman.

"Well done, Paucus," continued Lord Edom, somewhat patronizingly, "now, we need to do the same for Schwarzstein and Urganov; let's find some catchy names just like 'Paucus,' but not from the Latin, rather from the Old Slavic, something simple that will stick in people's minds and convey a subtle message favorable to us."

"Well then," proposed Paucus, "how about 'Lyubomir Tauragski,' after the Lithuanian city of Taurage; Lyub Tauragski, for short?"

Lord Edom nodded. "I like that name, Lyub," he said, "because, although Slavic, it sounds to Western ears like *lupus*, Latin for 'wolf', and Taurage suggests *taurus*, Latin for 'bull.' Very good. We need the fangs of a wolf and the horns and drive of a bull. But stick with the short form."

"Yes, 'Lyub Taraski,' sounds better," remarked Vogel, "because Lyubomir Tauragski is a tongue-twister for non-Slavs, including myself!"

"Lyubomir in Old Slavic," explained Safirberg, "means 'one who loves the world.'"

"A name well chosen," remarked Lord Edom. "We want our Lyubomir to spread socialism around the world! Socialism concentrates capital in the hands of the state, where we can directly benefit from it, through partnerships with the new authorities, who, to a man, will owe their seats to us! Call it state-owned if you will, but we will control it all."

"And what about Urganov?" asked Vogel. "What *nom de guerre* might we give him?"

"How about choosing for him a name drawn from Roxolan nature, something all people would recognize right away?" suggested Gondol.

"Well, how about," proposed Safirberg, "a name derived from the Ural River: Uralin."

"I like that: Uralin!" said Lord Edom, "Strong, masculine."

"Well then," said Safirberg, "so we have our two spearheads for the so-called vanguard of the proletariat: Taraski and Uralin."

"Good, now that we have names for them — Taraski and Uralin," asked Lord Edom, "what will they *do* for us, Gondol?"

"Well, here is my suggested plan," confided Gondol, "you gentlemen are invited, of course, to add to it or propose changes. But for good luck, repeat after me, *Rivalutsiya v Roxolanye! — Revolution in Roxolana!* That is the rallying cry promoted by my charity in New Lynden, the Society for Roxolan Freedom."

3. REFORMING ROXOLANA

<u>Imperial Palace, St. Paulusburg, November 1911</u>

True to form, his wounded hand in a bandage and his arm in a sling, Prime Minister Stolbetsin was soon back in his office at the Imperial Palace in St. Paulusburg. The first appointment of his day was with the finance minister, who had acted for him as head of government in his absence.

"I hope you didn't get too comfortable in my chair, Vitaly Nikandrovich!" said Stolbetsin with a smile. "You knew, of course, that I was coming back?"

"Pavel Arsenievich," replied the finance minister, "I prayed for your recovery from the moment I learned of the attempt on your life. No worries, I have enough on my plate with the finance portfolio. I have no wish to take on your portfolio permanently."

"Speaking of finance, Vitaly Nikandrovich, that is the prime constraint on our twenty-year plan of reform. All Western capital markets seem closed to us. The Cabal appears to have pulled shut all purse strings. What are our options?"

"Our output of gold continues to be the best way forward, Pavel Arsenievich. We sell the gold on the world market to pay for the imports we need."

"Yes, but the output of gold is too slow for the pace of our reforms and the Tsar does not want us to increase taxes for fear of causing more social unrest. Are all capital markets truly shut for us?"

"There are bankers from outside the Tribe who might lend to us, Pavel Arsenievich, but when it comes to Roxolana, they seem to act in concert with the tribal bankers for fear of reprisals for breaking ranks with the banking cartel."

"Yes, that is my assessment too. Nevertheless, we shall have to find a definitive way out to finance the twenty-year program. His Majesty expects a solution and quickly, because as we plan reform, there are those outside the country, and inside, who are actively planning and financing a revolution, *rivalutsiya*."

"What a horrid word, *rivalutsiya*!"

"I, too, prefer 'reform' to '*rivalutsiya*'!"

"There is a way to prevent revolution, Vitaly Nikandrovich."

"Indeed?"

"Yes," said Stolbetsin "if we were to grant a hard-working peasant a separate plot of land, ensuring water and using proper cultivation methods, then he would evolve into an independent, prosperous farmer, and, most importantly, a responsible, God-fearing citizen, grateful to his Tsar for the God-given order of things. He would not feel the need to overthrow the system."

"That's for the peasants, Pavel Arsenievich, but what about the Mazar revolutionaries?"

"We need to lift the restrictions on the Mazars, Vitaly Nikandrovich."

"Lift the restrictions that Tsar Andrei III put into place for a very good reason?"

"What was that very good reason, in your opinion?"

"Well, everyone knows that with their talent, drive, and clannishness, the Mazars take over anything and everything that they can lay their hands on, any organization, even the government, from the inside or, if they are on the outside, by revolution. Only strict restrictions can keep them in their place."

Pavel Arsenievich shook his head. "Look at the West, Vitaly Nikandrovich. We cannot copy everything from the West, but perhaps in the matter of their policy towards the Mazars, we might learn a thing or two. I am firmly convinced that it is better to have the Mazars inside our tent shouting out of it rather than outside our tent shouting into it. We must coopt them.

"Perhaps, we might appoint a few prominent Mazars to the public service, perhaps expand admittance quotas in universities and lift restrictions in the professions, allowing Mazars to practice law in their name, for instance, instead of under the name of an Orthodox Yeshuan lawyer. Many things are possible. We must reflect further."

"His Majesty and the aristocracy will never agree to relax restrictions on the Mazars. You will make even more enemies among the powerful and mighty, Pavel Arsenievich, by suggesting such a policy."

"I have plenty of enemies already, Vitaly Nikandrovich, among the mighty and the not-so-mighty. Yet, I have survived nineteen attempts on my life, no less, my friend. The angel of death refuses to come for me." Stolbetsin looked upwards and crossed himself. "The Lord has given me a holy mission to accomplish here and my time to go has not yet come. Anyway, this is a talk to be continued another day, but that is how I feel and for what I will work, even if it takes a long time. The safe future of Roxolana depends on it."

4. THE PEACE PILGRIMS

Lynden, Kingdom of Pryden
January 1914

The large chapel at Edom Court, an 18th-century manor house in the fashionable district of Lynden called River Fields, was lit with oil lamps. Tall stained-glass windows depicted in Art Nouveau style scenes from West Asian mythology that celebrated the victory of matter over spirit.

On a large altar rose an ancient statue of the god *Ballum*, the bringer of worldly power and wealth, who had been worshiped by the Sumerians and Akkadians as well as other peoples since then both in the Near East and the West. From burners on the altar there wafted through the room the aroma of frankincense.

The multicolored hand-painted ceramic floor tiles traced a pentagram. At each point of the five-pointed star, was placed a medieval carved wooden chair. Two points of the star were directed to either side of the altar. On the point of the pentagram furthest away from the altar stood a large, elaborately carved throne, whose occupant would face directly the image of *Ballum* and gaze directly into the eyes of the statue — two rubies that glinted red in the flickering light.

▲ ▲ ▲

At midnight sharp, a gong resounded through the hall, the great double doors directly across from the altar opened and five masked figures marched slowly in dressed in silk robes – the first in red with gold embroidery followed by four in black with no adornments.

The five figures took their seats at the five points of the pentagram and meditated in silence for a long while. Then organ music resounded through the chapel, an eerie tune in a minor mode, with a haunting motive. Perfectly in tune, the five hummed along in four-part harmony, with Red Robe and another who were tenors carrying the melody. Their vocalese resounded through the superb acoustics of the hall.

Suddenly, the music stopped. After a brief pause, Red Robe traced the sign of the pentagram across his chest and then chanted in Aramaic, "*Shlama Ballumah Gavrah*, hail to thee, *Ballum, Gavor*, great one, bringer of glory and gold through gore, through the power of thy pentagram grant us success in our enterprise."

The other four repeated the salutation, "*Shlama Ballumah Gavrah*." They intoned it to the creepy tune in four-part harmony and then sat silently for a long while in deep meditation, communing with the god *Ballum*. The gong resounded again and all rose and began to march anticlockwise over the points of the pentagram and chant as the organ picked up the weird melody again, once in A major and then in A minor, returning finally to A-major:

> *"Gavor, Gavor, gold and glory*
> *Great god, grant us gold and glory*
> *Gore for gold and gold for glory,*
> *Gavor, grant us guts for glory."*

The five sat down again, the organ went silent, and Red Robe took the floor.

▲ ▲ ▲

"The twentieth century must remain a Prydenian century," announced Red Robe, the masked Lord Nissim Edom. "If it does, great spoils await us all as peace pilgrims."

He paused for a moment, scanned their masked faces, and then went on, "But these riches will not come to us for free. In return, we will have to grant *Gavor* a great war, maybe two, in which many tens of millions of lives, both civilian and military, will need to be sacrificed to him."

They all hummed in unison the ghastly minor-mode melody and made the sign of the inverted pentagram on their chests.

"Grand Master, has *Gavor* demanded a figure of us?"

Red Robe nodded, "*Gavor* has demanded at least eighty million lives by mid-century, in however many wars and battles it may take. There will have to be a great war to begin this coming year that will last some four years and in the resulting peace must lie already the seeds of yet another war. In the twenty years between the wars will come a time of great prosperity, then a financial crash, which will bring a few of us much gold. Then the stage will be set for a second war, much bigger, much bloodier, which will complete the figure of eighty million lives sacrificed for *Ballum Gavor*."

They went silent, pondering the ideas their Grand Master had just shared with them.

"But out of war comes peace," said the black-robed figure to Lord Edom's right, Prydenian Prime Minister Sir Hubert Ashmore, with a smirk below his masked eyes, "the peace we piously serve as pilgrims."

"*Ex bello pax*," added a second black robe, War Minister Lord Robert Halberd. "Out of war comes peace."

"Indeed," replied Lord Edom. "*Ex bello pax*."

They all intoned together again in perfect harmony the catchphrase of the Peace Pilgrims set to the ghastly tune.

"Share with us the game plan that *Ballum Gavor* has revealed to you, Grand Master," said the prime minister.

"What a pity," remarked Lord Edom wistfully, "that Ripley is no longer with us. How I miss at times his verve and passion."

"Good old Barebone!" observed another black robe, the financier and lobbyist for African investments, Sir Arthur Milton, who had worked closely with Ripley over two decades. "Felled at the tender age of forty-nine."

In his last will, written in 1877, Sir Cyril Barebone Ripley, an adventurer, explorer, and mining magnate, had left his enormous fortune, built on gold and diamond mines in Prydenian South Africa, to the Peace Pilgrims charity, designating as his executors the five men around the pentagram, with the simple mission of strengthening, through private initiatives, the *Pax Prydenia*, the empire of Great Pryden, such that the sun would continue never to set on it. Ripley's stated last wish was to bring the entire world under Prydenian rule, including all of Africa, Midrealm, Reben, South Vespucia, and North Vespucia. For this purpose, his legacy would be a secret society. The Peace Pilgrims' Society was a murky organization that convened both at Edom Court, the home of Lord Edom, as well as in a townhouse which had once belonged to Sir Barebones Ripley, adventurer and mining magnate who had built his fortune in Southern Africa. Founded in 1900, when Ripley was still alive, the Peace Pilgrims, legally a charity, was aimed at fulfilling the terms of Ripley's will.

▲ ▲ ▲

Ripley's last will said little about how the society would meet its goal of promoting the *Pax Prydenia*. Presumably, the executors knew exactly what to do, based on further secret instructions that had not been made public. The head executor and consequently the chair of the secret society, to be called the Peace Pilgrims, was Lord Nissim Edom, a fabulously wealthy banker, whose family had made its fortune in the 18th and 19th centuries lending to kings, princes, and to both sides in numerous wars.

In reality, Ripley had been a mere agent of Lord Edom, and the funds that had come into the Peace Pilgrims foundation belonged to Edom himself and he had the final word on how every penny was spent.

The press had reported that Ripley had died naturally in 1902 from heart failure, but no one knew the truth. It was rumored that Ripley had outlived his usefulness to Lord Edom, who had obtained from the younger man all he needed, including the authentic Prydenian-sounding brand name, Ripley, under which to continue his extraction of African resources and conduct apparent philanthropy.

The charity work of the Peace Pilgrims included the brainwashing of generations of young world leaders through Ripley scholarships to Pryden's prestigious Kewford university, both Ripley's and Edom's *alma mater*, where several Ripley chairs had been endowed to impart the values that the Peace Pilgrims preached.

Some said that when Edom reckoned that Ripley had grown too big for his boots, the banker had Ripley's doctor, during a routine check-up, administer secretly to the adventurer, an otherwise healthy and athletic outdoorsman, a drug that simulated natural heart failure.

"But his legacy lives on," said Grand Master Lord Edom. "We, the Peace Pilgrims, embody it."

The four black robes exclaimed, "Hear, hear!"

"Pilgrims, we are at a juncture," continued Lord Edom, raising his palm to silence the others, "when a mere spark can ignite a Great War, such as the world has never seen."

"We have been anticipating such a war, Grand Master," said the war minister, "and building up the fleet and a massive expeditionary force capable of fighting on the Continent."

"Nothing your ministry has anticipated," snapped Lord Edom, "can match what will in fact happen."

"Let the Grand Master finish, Sword-bearer," chided the prime minister, using the war minister's code name.

"Certainly, Primus," replied the war minister, using the Prime Minister's code name, *Primus inter pares*, "first among equals."

"A series of carefully staged events must take place," resumed Lord Edom, "and their timing is everything." He looked fixedly at Foreign Secretary Sir Edmund Graves. "Your role, Globe-trotter, and that of your staff here and overseas will be crucial. There will be arms to twist and a broad public to deceive, both here and abroad. The public needs a motive grave enough to incense them into sending their sons, husbands, and fathers into battle as cannon fodder."

Graves nodded deferentially.

Lord Edom turned to the fourth black robe, Sir Arthur Milton, "And you, Gnome-of-the-dark, as always, will be the silver thread that connects all the dots."

Sir Arthur nodded, "Yes, Grand Master."

"Now for the invoice, as all good businessmen say," said Lord Edom. "It is time to speak of the price tag and who will pay."

The four looked intently at him.

"As always," continued Edom, "my bank and I will provide seed capital, but the main funding must, of course, come from the Exchequer, the national treasury.

"Our money man, the Chancellor of the Exchequer, is not part of our inner circle of pilgrims although he is in the first circle of pilgrims beyond our core group. So, I will ask Primus to brief us on how taxation will evolve."

"Our plan, Grand Master," said Primus, "is to increase the standard rate of income tax, which is 6 percent now to 30 percent over the next few years. The higher income tax will fund the war and permit the servicing of the huge government debt that the war will occasion."

"Yes, but do ensure that the 30 percent is reached within two to three years, not more, otherwise debt service will become an issue. We want interest paid from taxes not merely from more debt."

"We expect also," said Prime Minister Ashmore, "a substantial rise in the number of people paying income tax. Currently, the figure is only 1.13 million. Over the next few years, it should rise to 3 million. We plan, as the war progresses, to consolidate all the accumulated income tax legislation into a single act of parliament."

"I will do all in my power for crown and country," continued Lord Edom, "but in return, I expect something for my people, my tribe."

The prime minister, Primus, and the foreign secretary, Globe-trotter, knew what was coming because Lord Edom had discussed it with them many times in the past. But this was the first time that the secret society was signing off on the proposal. From now on, the government would have to deliver, or else there would be hell to pay.

"You mean a homeland for your people in West Asia, Grand Master," said the foreign secretary, "to be called 'Moledet.'"

"Precisely, Globe-trotter," said Lord Edom. "Moledet." He enjoyed having his wishes anticipated so that he appeared to be accepting tribute rather than making demands. "And remember we have agreed to call it a 'national home.' That phrase, with no precedent in international law, will allow us the ambiguity to define exactly what the name will mean in practice.

"Moledet will be a small plot of land compared to the ever-sunlit expanse of the Prydenian empire but a symbolically important area for my people, our homeland in the Good Book."

"Grand Master, it so happens that the land to be called Moledet," said the war minister, "is already densely inhabited by Badawi people, some eight-hundred thousand of them."

"That land," insisted Edom, "is the homeland of my tribe as indicated in the Good Book that is common to all of us — of both the Yeshuan and Mazar faiths. And those Badawi who feel uncomfortable with that will have to move out or be made to flee. The choice will be your government's."

The four black robes said, "Hear, hear! It shall be done!"

"Remember, as you sell the idea of Moledet to parliament, that the national home will serve not only my people but also the Prydenian empire as a trusty military and naval base in West Asia that will always be there to defend Prydenian strategic interests in a hostile region. Once the idea is sold to parliament, I shall expect a formal declaration from the foreign minister that His Majesty's Government views with favor the establishment of a national home for the Mazar people in the Holy Land. For now, in 1914, the prospect is too far away in time."

He looked around at the four black robes listening intently to him and continued:

"First, the Osmanli empire which controls the Holy Land will have to fall or be on the verge of falling, then as the *Pax Prydenia*, backed by our Gallic allies, stands perched to swallow the entire Eastern Mediterranean, Moledet will appear a viable proposition to the members of parliament.

"I estimate that the formal declaration of the national home should be made two or three years from now with the war in full swing and going Pryden's way. I shall assign my nephew, Maurice, to collaborate with the foreign office to draft the declaration."

"Moledet shall be your kingdom, Grand Master," said the foreign secretary.

Lord Edom shook his head. "I shall be merely the national home's humble steward, Globe-trotter, like the humble steward I am of the *Pax Prydenia*, just as we all are in the inner circle of the Peace Pilgrims."

All five of them knew, however, that even King Edmund VII of Pryden ultimately took his cues from Lord Edom, who, behind the scenes, controlled the Central Bank of Pryden and so also the empire's money supply.

"In the coming days," continued Lord Edom, "we will open our gatherings to members of the outer circles of the Peace Pilgrims. Our first set of meetings will be with those who forge the arms, then with those who shape public opinion, and finally with the lynchpins here and abroad who will bring about the chain of events to ignite this conflagration."

"Grand Master," said the Prime Minister, "you mentioned a war *or two*. Might you elaborate?"

"The transformations we require," replied Lord Edom, "may not all come about through one great war. For the *Pax Prydenia* to dominate the world, we would require two great wars, perhaps three, with long armistices in between. Rather than talking about it myself, I will ask Globe-trotter to brief us on the major transformations required, then the conclusions will become obvious."

"Prydenian domination of the world," said the foreign secretary, "is hindered by four empires — the Theudian, the Ostmark-Madjar, the Roxolan, and the Osmanli. We need the mother of all wars to destroy those four empires so that only the Gallic and the Prydenian are left, but the Gallic empire, too, is a rotting vine. So, we shall pull it down then invigorate it by grafting our empire onto it, especially in Africa and Southeast Asia."

All four others looked intently at him.

"We shall replace," announced Lord Edom, "big chunks of these four empires with small client statelets, barely viable, which will be dependent for their survival on the *Pax Prydenia*."

Nissim Edom paused for effect and looked at them one by one then continued: "Either their rulers will be autocrats propped up by Pryden or their borders will be so arbitrary, crossing ethnic lines, that there will be constant unrest, creating an opportunity for Prydenian interventions — diplomatic, financial, and military, as the case may be, either directly or through proxies."

The others all said, "Hear, hear."

"The four empires that I mentioned," resumed the foreign secretary, "are also in decline, just like the Gallic empire. The *Pax Prydenia* shall help herself to big slices of them."

"We must discuss the empires one by one, Grand Master," said Sir Arthur Milton, "if you will permit."

Lord Edom nodded, "That is why we of the inner circle are here, Gnome-of-the-dark. Now, Globe-trotter, give us your expert take on each of the empires. Others will then add to your observations."

"The autocratic emperors need to fall," announced the foreign secretary, "or our grand plan will not work."

"Is the transformation of these empires into tamer constitutional monarchies like ours, not an option?" asked the war minister. "After all, these monarchs are the cousins of our king."

"Brothers and cousins, too, have been known to kill each other, even in our Good Book," chuckled Lord Edom.

"Constitutional monarchies are not an option, Sword-bearer," replied the foreign secretary decidedly. "If those empires are to break up, the easiest means is to topple those emperors and replace their empires with many little republics, with disposable heads of state and government whose elections we can manipulate.

"What good would it do us to leave the monarchs in place? They would fight tooth and nail to keep their empires together. We need, rather, to feed the nationalisms that are bubbling throughout these four empires. It will be easy enough to do. Just stoke the fires a little."

"Our adventurers," added Sir Arthur Milton, an adventurer himself and friend of many others like the late Ripley, "the likes of Lord Barnham, a hero of Helvetian independence, and Africanists like Sir Cyril Barebone Ripley, Captain Sir Robert Buridan, and Dr. Legistowne possess the ability to go native and stir up the locals, convincing them that any revolution is all their doing, while, in reality, it is we, who are pulling the strings."

The five of them chuckled briefly.

"Still, deposing all these emperors seems an impossible task," said the war minister. "I think particularly of the Roxolan emperor. After all, he is Pryden's ally and first cousin of our king, as we just said. Yes, Grand Master, you reminded us that brothers even in our Good Book sometimes kill each other, but still..."

"Leave the fate of the Roxolan emperor up to my tribe, Sword-bearer," said Lord Edom with a broad smile. "He has it coming to him. Remember there are five million members of my tribe in Roxolana and he does not treat them well. So, they are furious with him and conjuring up a revolution — with a little help, of course, from me and my fellow bankers! But a precondition is war. If Roxolana can be induced to wage war, it will create a ripe environment for revolution."

"Among the Tsar's circle and in the press," concurred the foreign secretary, "they use the term Mazars and revolutionaries interchangeably. They assume now that all Mazars in their country are revolutionaries, overt or covert."

"And, they are not far off the mark!" commented Lord Edom. "We will have the Tsar toppled before you know it and our government will have little to do to obtain it. Leave it to my tribe to bring about. But, there again is another reason why our government owes my people a homeland in West Asia. My people will deliver Roxolana to the West on a platter. In return, Pryden will deliver to my tribe a national home in West Asia."

5. BREWING UP A WAR

"The *Entente*, our 'understanding' with Gallia and Pryden for mutual assistance and protection is a fool's errand, your Majesty," said Prime Minister Stolbetsin to the Tsar, "one cannot rely on it, nor on the 1907 Prydeno-Roxolan Agreement."

The Tsar frowned impatiently but Stolbetsin continued:

"Remember, Majesty, what that adventurer Norbert Bonacasa called the Prydenians: *les perfides Albions*. That is what they are. They are like weathervanes in the wind, pursuing only their interests. Remember the Crimean war.

"So, Majesty, never trust the Prydenians. And as for the Gallics, they are seeking revenge on Theudaland after they lost the war of 1870. But, alone, the Gallics cannot deter the Theudians. So, they wish to use Roxolana to threaten Theudaland with a two-front war."

"What alternative do you propose, Pavel Arsenievich?"

"We must revive the *Dreikaiserbund*, Majesty, the Three-Emperors-Alliance."

"Would Willy want that?"

"I think the Kaiser would, Majesty. Meet him at his favorite spa Bad Hohenburg, as you used to do in the past, where no one would suspect an alliance in the offing."

Bad Hohenburg lay close to Theudaland's border with Gallia and, like Elisaz and Lutringen, had been at different periods of history either Gallic or Theudian. Apart from its mineral springs, in continuous use since the days of the Latin empire, the spa represented a constant provocation to the Gallics that the Kaiser enjoyed making.

"What about Freddy? How do we bring the Ostmarkians in?"

"Invite the Ostmarkian emperor, too."

"Wouldn't the press be suspicious??"

Stolbetsin shook his head. "Merely three emperors having a holiday together."

"What about my father's commitment to the Gallics?"

"The Roxolan-Gallic agreement is a secret one."

"But on paper, still."

"Agreements can be changed, Majesty. It is no alliance. Let's not risk war because of Elisaz and Lutringen or Bad Hohenburg. That is not our fight. We have a country to reform. As I always repeat, give me twenty years of peace, without foreign entanglements, and I will give you a new Roxolana. You will not recognize it."

"You keep saying that, Pavel Arsenievich."

"Keep the banksters and the warmongers at bay, Majesty, and you will get it."

"Wolbozsky is very much in favor of the *Entente* with Gallia and Pryden."

Wolbozsky, the Tsar's ambassador to the Gallic Republic, had long since fallen out with Stolbetsin for fundamental differences in their world views and personalities.

"Your Majesty, with all due respect, Wolbozsky was responsible for the fiasco over Bassia-Herzogia."

In a secret meeting in 1908, Wolbozsky, at the time foreign minister of Roxolana, and the then Ostmarkian foreign minister, Count von Würdenthal had agreed to support each other in the following way: Ostmark would annex Bassia-Herzogia while Roxolana would declare the Straits of the Bosporus and Dardanelles as open to Roxolan naval ships. Wolbozsky did not, however, inform his superiors of this bold agreement. When the arrangement was made public, it nearly brought Europe to war.

The Illyrians, who had long considered as their own the neighboring Slavic territory of Bassia-Herzogia, began to mobilize for military action. Ostmark moved troops to the Illyrian border. Roxolana expressed its support for Illyria and Pryden supported Roxolana. Theudaland stood behind Ostmark. In the end, both sides in the confrontation backed down, but Ostmark retained its new territory of Bassia-Herzogia and Roxolana got nothing because no other powers recognized Roxolana's claim to the straits. Following this embarrassment, Wolbozsky began actively to support Illyrian nationalism.

The Tsar raised his palm to stop Stolbetsin and said:

"I could not drop Wolbozsky, Pavel Arsenievich. His family has loyally served my House of Tretyrimov for centuries. You, Pavel Arsenievich happen to have fallen out with him."

"He has fallen out with me, Majesty. He sees me as too

nationalistic, too attached to Roxolana."

"As you should be, but Wolbozsky does see well the European perspective."

"Your Majesty, Wolbozsky is a warmonger. His close fraternizing with Pryden and Gallia will only get us into an unwanted war. Wolbozsky wants to undo his humiliation by the Ostmarkians by launching a war with the Triple Alliance."

"Cut him some slack, Pavel."

"Majesty…." said Stolbetsin. "If there were to be a war — and your Majesty would be well advised to do all to prevent it — Wolbozsky would feel it was *his* war."

"Come, now Pavel. Give him some credit. He is an esteemed ambassador of ours."

"Majesty, Wolbozsky is too protective of Gallia's interests; he acts as if the territories of Elisaz and Lutringen, which the Gallics lost to the Theudians, were a Roxolan strategic interest, which, of course, they are not. He has 'gone native' since he went to Gallia in 1910. He defends Gallic interests more than ours."

"That will be enough, Pavel Arsenievich."

"Your Majesty." The prime minister bowed, took leave of the Tsar, and made his way back to his office.

Stolbetsin was very suspicious of Wolbozsky and Bernhartdorf, the Roxolan ambassador to Pryden, who were respectively in bed with the Gallics and the Prydenians and were pushing for the Triple *Entente*, an agreement which Stolbetsin saw as a big trap. Wolbozsky and Bernhartdorf both supported unconditionally the Triple *Entente*, advocated the costly rearmament of Roxolana, and backed Illyrian nationalism as a bludgeon to brandish at the Ostmark-Madjar empire. Wolbozsky used embassy funds to support the nationalist press in Gallia and was rumored to have funded the assassination of pacifist activists and politicians.

Unlike Wolbozsky, Stolbetsin did not believe in Greater Illyria nor expansionist Illyrian nationalism, nor in excessive Roxolan rearmament which diverted precious resources away from the social and economic progress of the Roxolan people.

Stolbetsin believed, instead, that a hard border was needed in the Balkans between the Ostmarkian empire and the Kingdom of Illyria, which both sides would recognize as a red line not to cross without risking war with Roxolana. Both sides would need to define what it meant to declare to the other, 'thus far and no further.' As Stolbetsin saw it, there were other priorities for the peoples of Europe than war, something which only benefitted the moneylenders and the arms manufacturers.

Stolbetsin saw Wolbozsky, Roxolana's ambassador in Lutecia, as a dangerous *provocateur*, someone who would do anything to promote a war between Gallia and Theudaland. The Tsar's intelligence service, the *Okhrana*, had reported to Stolbetsin that Wolbozsky was planning the assassination of a prominent socialist and pacifist Gallic member of parliament called Jacques Jeannot. Jeannot was dead-opposed to the Triple *Entente* and to any revanchist war with Theudaland to recover Elisaz and Lutringen. For his part, Wolbozsky simply wanted Jeannot dead.

For Stolbetsin, on the other hand, the only way to prevent war was for the Tsar to get closer to the other two emperors and revive the *Dreikaiserbund*.

Stolbetsin, whose wife and in-laws were of Germanic descent, had experienced in the Germanic cultures of Theudaland and Ostmark significant predictability and honesty that contrasted with the fickleness of the frivolous Gallics and the treacherous self-centeredness of the Prydenians. Added to this spicy *borsch* soup were venal warmongering arms merchants, Mazar bankers anxious to indebt Roxolana, and vainglorious generals.

What of the Roxolan peasant? Should he go to die for the goals of others, for the territories of Elisaz and Lutringen coveted by the revanchist Gallics, and for the Prydenian goal of destroying its naval rival, Theudaland? Why did the Prydenians refuse the friendship of the Kaiser? Why did they not accept the division of labor — Theudaland as the continental power and Pryden as the maritime power? There was a simple explanation — the Covert Cabal wanted war, the destruction of Theudaland, Ostmark-Madjaria, the Osmanli Empire, and Roxolana to leave the *Pax Prydenia* as the only empire on earth, the better to promote their financial interests. But Stolbetsin's slogan to warn against Prydenian and Gallic treachery was to repeat, "Never forget the Crimean War!"

Edom Court, Lynden, Kingdom of Pryden, May 1914,

"Gentlemen," announced Lord Edom, "The prospect of a great war looms before us, which will mean enormous profits for all of us."

"Hear, hear!" said the motley crew of arms manufacturers, bankers, and other war profiteers.

"Let me share with you some figures based on the estimates of our experts here and on the Continent. The Prydenian minister of war will brief us."

"With pleasure, *milord*," said Robert Halberd.

There was silence in the room as all hung on the Prydenian war minister's words.

"Let us consider just shells," said the war minister. "In the first five months of a possible war, once Pryden enters the conflict, I estimate that some half a million shells will be fired from Prydenian guns. With the progress of the war, after the general mobilization on all sides — and we will make sure that it becomes a prolonged and trigger-happy trench conflict — in the first full year of the war, I estimate that the Prydenian side alone will fire over sixteen-and-a-half-million shells."

"Attractive figures," said Heinz von Klopp, nephew of the Theudian steel magnate. "Our estimates for Theudaland are as follows."

All eyes turned to Klopp.

"We in Theudaland are raw-materials challenged, particularly for some of the elements required for high-grade steel for which we hold the patents, some of which we license to your arms manufacturers."

"Tell us, Count von Klopp, where you stand today," said Lord Edom.

"We, in Theudaland today," replied von Klopp, "hold an industrial advantage over both Pryden and Gallia. We are leaders in steel production, and in many branches of chemicals and engineering – and, with the outbreak of war, we estimate our output of shells just in 1914 would reach at least 1.36 million shells."

There were admiring gasps. Lord Edom nodded appreciatively, for he was also, through the Theudian branch of the Edom Bank, a large shareholder cum creditor of Klopp Steel.

Klopp junior continued, "But shortages of vital raw materials — particularly cotton, camphor, pyrites, and saltpeter — would mean that we will not be able to expand our production in Theudaland at the same rate as you in Gallia and Pryden who are building up stockpiles from your colonial network which is vaster than Theudaland's. We estimate that as the war progresses, just under 9 million shells would be made in 1915."

"Still an eight-fold increase over 1914," said Lord Edom. "Not bad at all."

"Nevertheless," continued von Klopp, "with some coordination, and the creation of a wartime raw materials department, as my uncle is proposing to the Kaiser, it should prove possible to commandeer stockpiles, allocate distribution, and, most importantly, oversee the chemical industry's production of synthetic substitutes."

"How would it then be in 1916, if we can bring about a trench-warfare stalemate?"

"We estimate that by 1916," replied von Klopp, "with the coordination of raw materials and expansion of synthetic materials, the production of Theudian shells can further increase by four to some thirty-six million."

"Brilliant!" exclaimed Lord Edom, calculating mentally what thirty-six million shells would bring him in dividends through his shares in Klopp Stahlwerke A.G.

"But just at the level of resources, in the longer term, our Central Powers — Theudaland, Ostmark-Madjaria, Osmali Empire, and Bilguria — cannot hope to compete with the *Entente's* financial and industrial muscle."

"But come, come, young Klopp," said Lord Edom, avuncularly rather than patronizingly, "your family will come out handsomely, no matter which side wins, with the cross-holdings of shares and the licenses for which Prydenian companies pay you."

"Yes, but what of Theudian honor, Lord Edom?" said the younger Count von Klopp grimly. "What of the Kaiser's dynasty, the House of Hochturm?"

"Look to your bottom line, young man," said Lord Edom sternly. "Kings and honor come and go, but fortunes remain. Remember your von Klopp family fortune dates back to the year 1587; it is even older than our Edom fortune. How many kings have come and gone since then? But the Klopps and their fortune are still here. Your family's fortune survived the first Thirty Years War of the seventeenth century, and it surely shall this second, far more profitable, Thirty Years War."

"What are your experts' estimates of total war expenditures for the Triple *Entente* side, Lord Edom?" asked von Klopp.

Lord Edom turned to the war minister, "Tell us, Halberd."

The war minister, Robert Halberd, said, "I can tell you, in all confidence, that we estimate the *Entente* will spend, in all, some 147 thousand million *talents* over the expected four or five years of the war."

"On our side," said von Klopp, "we estimate expenditures for the Triple Alliance of just under 62 thousand million *talents*, perhaps 61 thousand five hundred million *talents*, which is less than half of the *Entente's*."

"Well, well," said Lord Edom, "between all of us that makes for over 200 thousand million – to be precise, some 208 thousand, five hundred million *talents*."

"That includes, of course, soldiers' wages and foodstuffs," said the war minister, "not just armaments and war supplies."

"So much the better," said Lord Edom. "Some of us control conglomerates for food, textiles, and the like. At the end of the day, even soldiers' wages need to be spent on consumer goods. And of course, whatever they save comes into our banks as savings balances, which can serve us as the basis for expanding credit.

"Needless to say, the Edom family has branches in Gallia, Theudaland, Ostmark, and the Osmanli Empire and will continue, as they always have, to lend money to both sides in any war."

"You have all your contingencies covered, Lord Edom," replied von Klopp.

"As do most of you, gentlemen, even if not as fully as the Edom family. Now that we have looked at the financials of an upcoming war, let's discuss briefly how the war might come about. I want to hear from young von Klopp before all of the others because the role of Theudaland is crucial. It is said that the von Klopp family is the second head of Theudaland after the Kaiser himself!"

"With due respect, Lord Edom," replied von Klopp, "I would not go so far. Our family has armed the Kaiser's House of Hochturm for four centuries. We are their iron and steel smiths and armorers, no more, no less."

Lord Edom smiled, "Well, Mr. Smith and Armorer, please go on with the prospects for war."

"The mood in our capital, Berstadt, among the top brass and businessmen, is hawkish, Lord Edom, despite powerful doves in the government and civil society. Our supreme commander Alexander von Dubinke says we have a window of opportunity now to attack the *Entente* that will disappear in two or three years because of how Roxolana is rearming.

"With Roxolana's superior numbers of men and materiel and their legendary ability to retreat East beyond the Urals, as in the case of Norbert Bonacasa's 1812 invasion, we of the Triple Alliance will be inferior to them in two years. To grab what we can of Gallic and perhaps Roxolan territory, the time is now."

"Very good," said Lord Edom. "So, you are searching for a pretext for war. Others can help with that. Let's now hear from Ostmark. How does it look there, Berchtwald?"

"Well," said the Ostmarkian foreign minister, Count von Berchtwald, "our flashpoint with Roxolana is in the Balkans, as well as in the capital of the Osmanli Empire where the Theudians, through their support for the Osmanlis, are provoking Roxolana. Roxolana, of course, backs to the hilt Illyria which has dreams of a greater Illyria that would impinge on our empire in the Balkans.

"When we annexed Bassia-Herzogia in 1908, the Roxolans, perhaps still reeling from their Pacific adventure with the Kingdom of Reben, did not react militarily but only made loud noises. Our top brass and many at court would like to annex Illyria as soon as possible before they make further moves towards a greater Illyria. But the big question is how boldly would Roxolana react now that it has rearmed considerably since the end of the war with Reben in 1905. We wish to begin our annexation with a heavy bombardment of Plavigrad, the Illyrian capital at the confluence of the Danube and the Sava rivers. Of course, we still need a good reason to bombard them, perhaps the assassination of an Ostmarkian personality could be arranged, perhaps a provincial governor of noble descent."

"Who opposes such a bold plan?" asked Lord Edom.

"Our most vocal and powerful opponent," replied the Ostmarkian foreign minister, "is the heir to the throne, the *Thronfolger*, Archduke Felix Friedrich. He is our biggest and most powerful dove. What's worse, Lord Edom, he is nominally the head of the armed forces."

"Well, there you have it," replied Edom.

"Whatever do you mean, Lord Edom? What do we have?"

"You need a pretext to bombard Plavigrad and then annex Illyria. Well, if you could arrange an assassination of the archduke and blame Plavigrad for it, you would have your *casus belli*."

"That is a long shot. The *Thronfolger* is well protected in Vedunia."

"I always think of 'short shots', not 'long shots'," said Lord Edom. "Does he not tour the empire regularly to inspect the deployed armed forces? Arrange the assassination while he is on tour. Where does he go next?"

"On 27 and 28 June of this year," replied the Ostmarkian foreign minister, "he is due to visit Saraybas, the capital of our recently annexed province of Bassia-Herzogia."

Lord Edom thought for a moment. "That just might work."

"Well, the city is crawling with nationalist Illyrians and anarchists," admitted the Ostmarkian foreign minister.

"I think through the ancient Stonecutters Guild we might be able to arrange a mishap," said Lord Edom.

"There are many in Vedunia who would lend this initiative support, many who would like to see the archduke out of the way."

"Let us meet separately from this meeting, Berchtwald, along with your Prydenian counterpart here, Sir Edmund Graves, to work out the details. I think we can arrange something that would serve as the tinderbox for our Great War. It would give you Ostmarkians a reason to attack Illyria, ostensibly in self-defense and for reprisals. The heavily rearmed Roxolans are sure to react, likely militarily, and you would then be able to draw Theudaland, your close ally, into the conflict."

"Our Theudian military has a plan, hatched by our late General von Holzweg, to address effectively a two-front war," explained von Klopp. "Theudaland would attack Gallia by moving an army through neutral Lotharia, smash Gallia, and then return to finish off Roxolana before Roxolana can deploy its full strength. We call it the Holzweg Plan."

"I like it," said Lord Edom. "Logical and rational, very Germanic."

"Our military intelligence has made us aware of the Holzweg Plan," said War Minister Halberd. "It is an open secret."

"Now, one step at a time, and in proper sequence," said Lord

Edom. "First, the *casus belli*, the assassination of the archduke, then a nice ultimatum to the Illyrians from the Ostmarkians, that will irritate the Tsar, bringing in the Roxolans. Then, the Ostmarkians, invoking the Triple Alliance, will draw in Theudaland and the rest should follow nicely. Once Theudaland attacks Gallia, Pryden will get all riled up."

"How likely is it that Pryden will enter the war?" asked von Klopp. "They could just sit it out."

"Pryden will not sit it out," revealed the Prydenian war minister. "The enlightened members of our government will make sure she will come in. Many of us are keen to see Pryden enter the war."

"But what about Eire?" asked von Klopp. "The rebellion you face in Eire? The Prydenians seem all tied up in Eire. Our military intelligence believes that Gallia will face Theudaland alone."

"That is the deception Pryden is operating," revealed the war minister. "We want the Theudian military to attack Gallia boldly, thinking that Pryden would not come to their ally's aid beyond moral support."

"I see," said von Klopp.

"At the same time," said Lord Edom, "we will need an effective provocation to bring Theudaland into the war, because the Theudians might prefer, despite their alliance with Ostmark, to see the Balkan crisis remain a local affair, something for Ostmark to tackle directly with Illyria. And they may not have an incentive to attack Gallia. One must be created."

"Indeed, we need to ensure, by hook or by crook, that Theudaland enters the war," announced von Klopp. "For there is still some resistance in the government, not least from the Kaiser, to start a new war. We had one already in the 1870s with Gallia. Many in my country ask, why another war? After all, we have gained the territories of Elisaz and Lutringen, plus we have Bad Hohenburg, the Kaiser's favorite resort that was held by Gallia in the past. What else do we need from Gallia? It is the Gallics who want Elisaz and Lutringen back, even though the people there speak a Germanic dialect, and the province is, therefore, by rights part of Theudaland. The top brass and the army purveyors such as ourselves, on the other hand, are very keen on a war."

"Perhaps," said War Minister Robert Halberd, "we in Pryden might be able to spook the Theudians into launching a preemptive attack against Gallia and Pryden."

"Just how would you do that, minister?" asked von Klopp.

"Oh simple," said the war minister, "we would send the mighty Prydenian fleet west to threaten your Baltic ports."

Von Klopp shook his head, "but the timing of all of this is so close, the sequencing so difficult. Will it work?"

Lord Edom smiled, "My dear young chap, our planning always has worked. Trust us; for over a century, since the Norbert Bonacasa wars, the Edoms in each generation, along with like-minded souls such as yourselves, have been organizing and funding wars! And how handsomely we have profited from those. Our profits from the upcoming war will dwarf those from previous conflicts."

"How will the war begin, and when?" asked Stavro Stavroff, the secretive sales agent of the Prydenian firm, Seagers Armaments, of which Lord Edom was the principal shareholder.

"It will all begin," announced the Ostmarkian foreign minister, Count Leonhard Berchtwald, "in Saraybas, an ancient oriental-style city in the Balkans, whose name means 'the inn by the running waters.' The plan hinges on the elimination of the biggest dove in the Ostmark-Madjar Empire. This is an event that we can convert into a case for war. The success of the rest lies largely in the hands of our present company, despite all the moving parts there are."

6. SARAYBAS

<u>Lynden, Pryden</u>
<u>26 June 1914</u>

Through a tall picture window at their exclusive day school, two curious young girls on their break watched the Foreign Office building across the street, where just outside the main gates a black Rolls-Royce Silver Ghost sedan was parked in a no-parking zone. The chauffeur stood distractedly on the sidewalk by the sedan car smoking, while the two policemen stood silently at attention on either side of the gate.

"What a lovely car," said the younger girl, with red hair and green eyes. "It's there every day right next to the gates in that no-parking spot. I wonder whom it belongs to?"

"That's Lord Nissim Edom's car," said the older girl, with dark brown hair and eyes.

"How do you know?" asked her companion.

"My family knows him; he is related to us."

"Does he live in that building?"

The older girl shook her head, "He lives at Edom Court in River Fields."

"But that car stands parked there nearly every day," the red-headed girl reiterated, "And for hours on end. I could have sworn the man lived in there."

The brown-haired girl let out a laugh. "No, he doesn't live there. But you might say he owns the place."

▲ ▲ ▲

The foreign secretary, Sir Edmund Graves, welcomed Lord Edom. The attendant took Lord Edom's top hat and cane and left the office. The banker settled down into the comfortable padded armchair in front of the foreign secretary's desk.

"What do you have for me today, Graves, what updates from Vedunia, Plavigrad, and Saraybas?"

Lord Edom made it a point to call him "Graves," rather than "Sir Edmund." In addition to the title of the third baronet of Graves that he had inherited, which allowed him the style of "Sir Edmund", the foreign secretary had also recently been made a "knight of the garter" by King Godfrey V, at the urging of Lord Edom, officially for services the foreign secretary had rendered to the empire, but in reality, for being the banker's loyal servant.

"*Milord*, the news is good and everything is lined up. Our operatives in Plavigrad, Vedunia, and Saraybas have all delivered as planned."

"Nothing ever goes exactly as planned, Graves," said Lord Edom, shaking his head. "Our bitter experience and failures in Roxolana have shown us that. But hopefully, things will go better in Saraybas."

"They will, sir. Trust me. There are fewer moving parts to this engine."

"Spare me the mechanical metaphors, Graves, and get on with it."

"First, from Plavigrad. Our double-agent Dimitri, of the Illyrian nationalist secret society, the *Crna Ruka* or Black Hand, has sent a ciphered cable, saying that all seven of their agents, including the leader of the task force, Ivić, have safely crossed the border into Ostmarkian Bassia-Herzogia. The seven men are all in place in the provincial capital, Saraybas. The agents will line the riverside quay at all the bridges as the car of the heir to the throne passes. Six of them will be ready to attempt a kill, as soon as feasible. They are all armed with grenades and semi-automatic pistols — Brownings, all made in the Kingdom of Lotharia at their Fabrique Nationale. These Western weapons — rather than Theudian or Ostmarkian ones — in the hands of the assassins will draw suspicion away from the Germanic side to ours, helping to implicate our *Entente*, particularly Lotharia which Theudaland will need to invade and cross to attack Gallia. In any case, once they make the kill, fingers will point to the Black Hand society and the Kingdom of Illyria. The top brass in Vedunia will have a pretext to start a war with Illyria. Roxolana would then enter the war on the side of its Slavic ally, Illyria, and oppose the *Entente*, bringing in Gallia and Great Pryden."

The *Entente* was the informal understanding that linked Great Pryden, Gallia, and Roxolana. It was not a formal alliance, unlike the Triple Alliance between Theudaland, Ostmark-Madjaria, and Latium, and the uncertain link in the *Entente* remained Roxolana. Lord Edom was skeptical of the *Entente* and knew that to bring about war, additional aggressive measures, including several false-flag operations and deceptions, would be needed to mobilize the three outer allies against the three central powers.

"What about the troops from the maneuvers?" asked Lord Edom, "Won't they come back from their exercises to protect the archduke? What good will it be to have assassins in the crowd if there are walled in by troops who can stop them at any moment?"

"Don't worry, sir. Our contacts in Vedunia in the high-command have seen to it that there will be no troops lining the riverside quay."

"What about the troops from the maneuvers? Won't they come back with the archduke?"

"The troops will deliberately not be supplied with the proper uniforms for ceremonial escort duty and that is the excuse the top brass will use for not deploying troops along the riverside quay after the maneuvers: wrong uniforms. The ceremonial uniforms have not even been shipped to the barracks in Saraybas. The archduke, a clotheshorse himself and a stickler for proper uniforms and protocol, will understand and concur right away."

"So, what is so special about the 28th of June? Why was that day chosen? In my culture, we ask once a year at a religious festival, 'why is this day different from other days?'"

"Well, sir, it is the day that the top brass of the Ostmarkian-Madjar empire deliberately selected for military maneuvers in Bassia-Herzogia. But there are several details about the date that make it significant."

"Really?"

"It happens to be the very day fourteen years ago when the archduke and former countess took an oath renouncing any claims by their descendants to the royal succession."

"Oath of Renunciation? Explain, Graves."

"As I said, sir, the archduke entered a morganatic marriage to the Bohemian countess Stepanka von Manželek, a noblewoman but not one of royal blood. Although the emperor has since granted her the courtesy title of Duchess of Hochwald, she is not allowed to accompany the *Thronfolger* to any official functions in Vedunia. Her children will not inherit the throne. So, he is taking her with him to Saraybas, where she will be given all the honors as if she were indeed a crown princess. She will be better treated there than at court in Vedunia, where she has to remain invisible."

"Wait a minute, Graves. If she cannot accompany the archduke on official tours, because she is a morganatic wife, how is she permitted to go to Saraybas with him? What is different about this trip?"

The foreign secretary beamed at the opportunity to patronize Lord Edom, who usually talked down to him, "because, sir, the archduke is going there as a military commander to oversee army maneuvers that the top brass has arranged precisely on this day. He is not going there in his royal capacity or to represent the emperor."

"I see that these details can be important to that sort of people. Makes little sense to me. Anyway, if I can help it, the archduke is not going to inherit the throne."

"Additionally, sir, from what we know from our spies among the hawkish, war-mongering top brass in Vedunia who, like us, want the dovish archduke out of the way, the 28th was chosen because it is St. Vitus' day, *Vidodan* in the local language."

Edom frowned. "Enlighten me, Graves, St. Vitus' day? That is not my religious tradition. I don't happen to keep saints' days in my head."

"Most significantly for the local people, *milord*, that is the day when the Osmanli forces in the fourteenth century conquered the Illyrians. An Illyrian soldier nonetheless crept into the sultan's tent and slit the ruler's throat, before the assailant was himself beheaded. So, we will have quite a few angry patriotic Illyrians afoot wanting to kill the heir to the Ostmarkian throne, just as their distant ancestor killed the sultan."

"Still, it all sounds too good to be true. Too many coincidences."

"Trust the process, sir. All the stars are truly aligned this time."

"Graves, if you see me today occupying the position I do, it is because I never have simply trusted processes nor left anything to chance or the stars."

Idilična Resort, 10 km from Saraybas,
8 a.m., Sunday, 28 June, 1914

"As you ordered, Your Imperial Highness," said the *maître d'hôtel* in the Hotel Bassia in the spa town of Idilična, some ten kilometers outside of Saraybas. On cue, the waiter uncovered the silverplate dome over the salver to reveal a typical breakfast of Bassia-Herzogia.

Archduke Felix Friedmar, heir to the throne of Ostmark-Madjaria looked at his wife Stepanka, Duchess von Hochwald. "For our fourteenth wedding anniversary, *Schatzl*, I thought I would surprise you by ordering a lavish Bassian breakfast instead of our usual Semmel rolls and croissants with Vedunian coffee.

"After all, Bassia-Herzogia is now formally part of our empire and just as we would have a Bohemian breakfast in your homeland or a Madjar breakfast in Madjaria, I thought it fitting for us to have a Bassian breakfast here."

The duchess smiled, "What have they prepared for us, *Friedl?*"

The archduke nodded to the *maître d'hôtel*, who explained, "To start, Your Imperial Highnesses, Bassian coffee."

The waiter poured out for the imperial couple two cups of coffee prepared with the grounds in a small *jizve* copper pot with a long ivory handle.

"Allow the grounds to settle and then sip it, my dear," suggested the archduke.

The duchess sipped the coffee, narrowed her eyes, and said, "It's strong, much stronger than our Vedunian coffee."

The *maître d'hôtel* then presented the various delicacies on the salver on the trolley next to their table: a meat and cheese platter with beef prosciutto, smoked sausages, Travnički cheese, Livno cheese, sour cream, and *uštipci* doughnuts along with cucumbers and tomato. For good measure, the restaurant had also included the familiar Semmel rolls and croissants.

After the maître and waiter had left, the archduke said, "We have a long day ahead of us, my dear, best to arm ourselves with a hearty breakfast."

The duchess tasted some of the local dishes but then picked up a Semmel roll, tore off a small portion, and put it delicately into her mouth.

"I'm not particularly hungry today," she said. "I have an uneasy feeling."

"But isn't it marvelous that we can be together in public like this on our wedding anniversary?" replied her husband, "Instead of playing hide-and-seek with the imperial protocol that won't let us be together in public in Vedunia?"

She nodded, "Yes, of course. But I have this eerie feeling that something is not quite right about today."

"Our anniversary, darling!"

"Yes, but also the date of our Oath of Renunciation."

"That, too, but our anniversary first."

"And it's the Illyrian national day, Vidodan, St. Vitus' Day. All the rebellious Illyrians will be up and about."

"Just another local feast day, darling."

"All in all, 28 June does not seem an auspicious day."

"That's superstition, my dear, *blose Aberglaube*. Don't worry; all will go well. And most importantly, I will have you beside me the whole day!"

"That's the best part of this trip. I am not leaving your side."

▲ ▲ ▲

Saraybas, 8.30 a.m.

In the corner of a small pastry shop near the quay along the river were gathered six young Illyrians and a young Bassian. At the head of the table was an older man who opened a large leather bag and began handing out bulky brown paper bags to the younger men.

"Hand grenades and fully-loaded Browning pistols for each of you."

He then handed out small white envelopes, the kind that pharmacists used to wrap medicinal pills. "Your cyanide capsules," the man explained. "Keep them in the lapel pockets of your jackets so that you can reach them quickly if you are about to be caught. Put the pill between your molars, bite hard, and swallow quickly. It is fast-acting."

They all nodded silently. They all knew what violent interrogations would await them at the hands of the Ostmarkian police if they were to be caught.

"To make this plan fool-proof, there are six of you, each one across from one of the bridges along the riverside quay. The bridges will provide you with a good escape route as most of the crowds will be standing on the sidewalk opposite the quay to avoid the sun. The bridges should be clear and would enable you to dash. You can also jump into the river if need be."

The young men were silent but some nodded.

"You know your stations; we have rehearsed this many times without the weapons. Now you have the weapons. This is no longer a dry run; this is the real thing. One of you must succeed in making the kill, either with a grenade or with one or more pistol shots. Once again, their special train is expected at the station at 9.50 a.m. The motorcade should enter the riverside quay around 10.00. They plan to reach City Hall by 10.15. Our job is to make sure they do not make it to City Hall."

They finished their Bassian coffee quickly, leaving behind the fortune-telling grinds at the bottom of the handle-less cups, and left, each one in a different direction. Had they had more time, they might have cast their fortunes with the coffee grinds.

▲ ▲ ▲

After breakfast, Archduke Felix Friedmar signaled to his secretary, who was awaiting his cue by the wall of the dining hall. The young man hurried over and the *Thronfolger*, the heir to the throne, said, "Take a telegram, Hermann."

The secretary nodded, taking up his pad and pencil.

"Address it to our daughter Stephanie: 'Mamma and I are very well. Weather warm and beautiful. We had a big dinner yesterday, a typical Bassian breakfast this morning. After mass, we head to Saraybas for a big reception in the morning. Big dinner again in the afternoon and then departure. Deep hugs and kisses. Pappa.'

The archduke waited as the secretary finished taking down the text in shorthand. Then he said, "Have it sent immediately as a top priority message."

"*Jawohl, Kaiserliche Hoheheit*," replied the secretary, "It will be done, Imperial Highness."

▲ ▲ ▲

Between Idilična and Saraybas, 9.45 a.m.

The *Thronfolger* and his wife looked out of the window of their special train at the Bassian countryside. It was a mere fifteen-minute ride from the resort of Idilična to the center of Saraybas, some ten kilometers away.

The archduke took out his gold pocket watch which contained a picture of his wife as a young woman. They were running seventeen minutes late because, after the Sunday Holy Mass in the Idilična church, where the priest had said a special blessing for them on their wedding anniversary, he had decided to take a romantic stroll back to the hotel with his beloved Stepanka rather than taking their carriage.

As Stepanka looked out of the window, Felix Friedmar admired her and then glanced again at her photograph in his watch case. She was forty-six years old now but had retained the beauty of her younger years. He recalled how this watch with her picture had changed his life.

It was some nineteen years ago, in 1895, when he was serving as a young officer in Bohemia, staying at the castle of his distant uncle, another archduke, a second cousin of the present emperor. He had first met Stepanka, the fourth daughter of a Bohemian count and ambassador, at a ball in Praha, the capital of Bohemia. She happened to be serving as lady-in-waiting to Archduchess Elise, the wife of his uncle.

To see Countess Stepanka again, he had taken to visiting his uncle's castle in Prehmišburg. His uncle's wife, Archduchess Elise, had been delighted because she assumed Felix Friedmar had fallen in love with her eldest daughter, Maria Margarete. She discovered the truth when she chanced upon this pocket watch that Felix Friedmar had left behind at the castle when he had left on a hunting trip with his uncle. When Archduchess Elise saw, instead of her daughter's picture, that of her lady-in-waiting, she was disappointed and incensed. She promptly sent Stepanka away.

Felix Friedmar stopped visiting his uncle's castle and declared his intention to marry Stepanka. There was opposition from the emperor because Stepanka, although of minor Bohemian nobility, was not of royal blood. Nevertheless, in 1899, the emperor relented and agreed to the marriage, on the condition that Felix Friedmar renounce all succession rights to the throne for any children from the union. Felix Friedmar accepted the condition. Stepanka and he were married in a private ceremony, which was ignored by all of the imperial court, except for his step-mother and her two daughters, who attended.

Court protocol, punctiliously enforced by the chief of protocol, himself the resentful son of a morganatic marriage, imposed petty humiliations on Stepanka, who could not accompany Felix Ferdinand to official events. Yet, never once did Felix Friedmar regret his marriage, which was a happy one that had produced three children, a fourth having been stillborn. After nearly two decades since they had first met, they were still very much in love.

The train began to slow down. It was almost 10.07 a.m. and they were about to arrive at Saraybas station. Following the arrival fanfare with the army band, there would be a very short visit to the largest barracks in the city, the defensive camp of the imperial troops in Bassia-Herzogia. Then, they would drive through the streets of Saraybas to City Hall for an official ceremony.

▲ ▲ ▲

It was a warm sunny day. The seven-vehicle motorcade, with the archducal couple in the third open touring car, made its way through the festively decorated streets of the city to the riverside quay which led to City Hall. Everywhere were banners welcoming the *Thronfolger* to Saraybas. The chauffeur drove swiftly at a speed of twenty-five kilometers an hour as he had been instructed to do for the security of the imperial visitors. But the archduke asked the driver to slow down, "I want to see the people clearly," he said. "At this speed, they are just a blur."

The chauffeur slowed to ten kilometers an hour and the archduke said, "That's better."

▲ ▲ ▲

The motorcade approached the Charcoal Bridge, so-called because, in Osmanli times, spent charcoal ashes would be thrown into the river from it. On the sidewalk directly perpendicular to the bridge, stood the first assassin, a young Bassian of the *Yielder* faith. He clutched at the hand grenade in his coat pocket and readied himself to pull the cap and hurl the object. Suddenly, someone jostled him from behind, trying to get a closer look at the archducal couple. In the packed crowd, the Bassian lost his nerve and did not withdraw the grenade from his pocket. The second assassin, an Illyrian standing close to the Bassian, when he saw that the duchess was sitting next to the archduke, also chose not to shoot or throw his grenade.

▲ ▲ ▲

Standing on the riverside of the quay closer to the Charcoal Bridge, the third assassin, an Illyrian named Nenad Karadzić, threw his hand grenade. The driver saw the flying object approaching and stepped on the accelerator. The grenade landed on the folded-back fabric top just behind the archducal couple, slid off, and fell on the road.

The object rolled on the street under the next vehicle in the motorcade, which had also accelerated and then exploded under the third car. Several officers from the escort unit were injured including a colonel. The explosion ripped a large hole in the road surface.

Gaining further speed, the driver delivered the archducal couple and the governor, who was with them in the car, safely to City Hall for the ceremony.

▲ ▲ ▲

The mayor of Saraybas delivered a prepared speech, without acknowledging the violence that had just taken place. In his reply, the archduke said that he had been greeted with a bomb attack, but was heartened by the jubilant ovations of the population, which he saw as an expression of joy at the failure of the attempt on his life.

Following the speeches, the aide responsible for the archducal couple's safety suggested having all the streets cleared of crowds. The archduke refused but said, "Simply cancel the reception and cut short the program, but I will go to the hospital to visit the wounded and then on to the station to board our special train back to Vedunia."

"Your imperial highness, after all these attempts on your life, I think it time to call off even the visit to the hospital and go directly to the station."

"I will do no such thing," replied the heir to the throne. "But take the duchess to the train station right away to await me. After the hospital, I, too, will head straight for the train station."

"As you wish, Imperial Highness."

"But *Friedl*," protested the Duchess of Hochwald, "my place is by your side — always. I will not go to the station alone to await you."

"With all these attempts on my life, dear, I cannot allow you to risk your life anymore. Think of our three children. You must always be there for them."

"So, I shall and so will you."

"I don't understand, my dear," replied the archduke. "You were the one who said the 28th of June was an unlucky day for us because that's when we took the Oath of Renunciation."

"And you were the one who said that this was a silly old superstition."

"So, I did."

"Well, I believe my husband and future emperor are right!"

The archduke shook his head and crossed himself. "Superstition or not, a prudent man dies old, as the folk wisdom says. And we are just being prudent."

The Duchess turned to the governor and exclaimed with a tone of finality, "As long as the archduke is in public today, I will not leave his side!"

▲ ▲ ▲

At 10:40 a.m., the motorcade with the archduke and duchess left City Hall and returned west along the riverside quay in the direction of the hospital which was in the city center. The governor sat on the jump-seat of the open touring car in front of the archducal couple. The governor had given instructions that, instead of taking the scheduled route using the thronged inside roads to the hospital and then the station, the motorcade would take the longer route, driving swiftly along the riverside quay to avoid any further incidents. However, the governor's instructions had not been relayed to the archduke's driver, who turned, as originally programmed, onto the side street that was the shortest route to the hospital and station.

"You're driving the wrong way," yelled the governor, turning back towards the driver, "We changed the route. We're supposed to go over to the riverside quay!" The chauffeur stopped and put the car into neutral to coast slowly back towards the riverside quay. The street was thronged on both sides with cheering crowds. When the car reached the riverside road, the driver brought the car to a full stop, turned the car around, and prepared to engage first gear. No one in the car noticed in the crowd on the sidewalk less than three meters away, the Illyrian assassin, Gradimir Pravić.

▲ ▲ ▲

Gradimir Pravić could not believe his eyes. Right in front of him, was the *Thronfolger's* car that had come to a full stop. Ignoring the bystanders, Pravić quickly drew his pistol and fired three times. The first bullet hit the governor in the abdomen; he immediately collapsed. As soon as he saw the shooter, the archduke, with the reflexes of a soldier, immediately pulled the duchess down out of harm's way. But, as he then ducked, he received the second bullet in the shoulder, which was protected by his bullet-proof vest. The third shot missed its mark. The archduke saw several bystanders seize and disarm the assassin. The driver threw the car into gear and sped along the riverside quay towards the hospital.

▲ ▲ ▲

"It didn't work, did it, Globe-trotter?" said Lord Edom to the foreign secretary, both wearing the masks and robes of their secret society.

"Grand Master, it almost did," replied the foreign secretary.

"Almost, is not good enough, Globe-trotter."

"There are still other resources."

"The governor was seriously wounded but will live," said Lord Edom. "The archduke and the duchess escaped harm and are safely back in Vedunia. The archduke's return to court is setting back and possibly hindering seriously the prospects for Ostmark waging war on Illyria."

"The final word has not been said yet, sir. We have aces up our sleeve. We can still eliminate him."

"No, there is more than one way to skin a cat. We need to find a better way to ignite this war, even with the archduke alive."

"The rest of the war party in Vedunia is still gunning for him, sir. We need only egg them on a little, or lend them a hand, and they will do him in."

"No, forget the archduke. Look at all the alternatives and come up with a plan. Meanwhile, let's also work on the other actors: Roxolana and Theudaland. What about right at home here. What are the plans for bringing Pryden into the war?"

The four others in black robes liked it when their grand master allowed them leeway to propose plans. Most of the time it felt like they were merely his errand boys.

Primus, Prime Minister Ashmore, took the floor. "Grand Master, our greatest trump card is the fact that officially our government is struggling with the political crisis in Eire, with the Eire Liberation Army throughout the island. We will saturate the press with stories of our government's frustration and involvement in Eire. So that no one will suspect that we have our eye on entering the conflict on the side of the *Entente*."

The Grand Master nodded. "I had heard of this deception before and I like it. Blindside the public, the Theudians, and the Ostmarkians. But what will bring about the war? What will be the actual motive for Pryden to enter the war?"

Globe-trotter, the foreign minister, spoke up: "The key to our entering the war with public acceptance will be when the neutral kingdom of Lotharia becomes the passageway for the Theudian army to come to face Gallia on the battlefield."

"What if neutral Lotharia simply allows the Theudian army to pass through, just as the Lusitanian colonies in Africa permitted Prydenian troops to pass through to get to South Africa during the Boer War?"

"That will not happen, Grand Master. We will ensure that Lotharia refuses the Theudians passage, forcing them to invade her. In any case, the King of the Lotharians has reportedly told the Kaiser that he will fight any army that comes in uninvited. We are in contact with the Lotharians."

"I like that," said the Grand Master, nodding.

"As the Theudians pass forcibly though Lotharia, our press will accuse them of atrocities against Lotharian civilians. The press will lay it on thick, saying the Theudian soldiers are raping and killing women and children and skewering Lotharian babies for bayonet practice. We can even stage some atrocities in a film studio, with plenty of dark dye for blood, not even red dye, since the images are black and white anyway."

The Grand Master nodded with a smile. "That's the way to do it!"

Gnome-of-the-dark, Sir Arthur Milton, added, "The Prydenian public will be so incensed they will cry out for the government to enter the conflict on the side of the Gallics who will be facing the Theudians after these have crossed through the gateway of Lotharia."

Sword-bearer, War Minister Robert Halberd, added, "We will run the wartime propaganda mill, producing posters to be placed in every train and underground train station: 'Avenge the Hun!' There will be a picture of a gorilla in a Theudian army costume, carrying a dead raped woman in one arm and a bayonetted baby in another. "Remember the rape of Lotharia!"

"I like it," said the Grand Master, "Let's agree on that course of action then."

7. TIME FOR WAR

<u>Tsar's Village, Roxolana, July 1914</u>

"What a relief that the archduke and the duchess escaped the attack," said the Tsar. "Pity about the governor, but he will live. What a motley collection of assassins, but luckily, they were incompetent adolescents. Even their cyanide pills were expired. The Ostmarkians are torturing all seven of them to obtain a rounded picture of the conspiracy."

"The Illyrians got what they wanted, a political statement through bloodshed, even if there were no deaths."

"Yes, but did the Cabal get what they wanted?"

"Probably not. They will try again."

"The archduke's death would have meant a serious confrontation between Ostmark-Madjaria and Illyria in the Balkans."

"It would have. This reminds me of my 'mishap' at the opera house."

"Doesn't it now? What good guardian angels you both have!"

"What good bulletproof vests, you mean, Majesty."

The Tsar let out a grim chuckle. "Keep wearing it."

"I shall wear it, Majesty, and hope that next time they don't aim for my head."

"What have you brought me, Pavel Arsenievich?"

"To hear all the implications of this crisis in the Balkans, would you like to summon the foreign minister?"

"I'd rather hear it from you, Pavel Arsenievich, rather than your brother-in-law, Samsonov. You tell it to me as it is. Nor would I want to hear it from a bunch of generals and ministers in hock to interests beyond Mother Roxolana. Least of all, from my ambassadors in Lynden and Lutecia, God bless them both!"

"I shall do my best, Majesty."

"Go on."

"Behind the assassination attempt is said to lurk the *Crna Ruka*, the notorious *Black Hand* secret society, committed to uniting all the

Slavs of the Balkans. The society's actual name and motto is *Ujedinenje ili smrt,* union or death."

"Who funds them, Pavel Arsenievich?"

"They are an organization with links to the freemasons, the related Stonecutters Guild, and other revolution mongers, among them the mysterious Peace Pilgrims of Pryden. The overthrow of monarchies is their aim, in both Illyria and Ostmark-Madjaria and even right here in Roxolana."

The Tsar did not react to the mention of Roxolana in the same breath as 'revolution.' He merely exclaimed, "Peace Pilgrims, indeed! What a cynical name!"

▲▲▲

"Even without the death of the archduke, we will be able to coax the Ostmarkian government into declaring war on Illyria," said Globe-trotter, Foreign Secretary Graves, dressed in his mask and black robe.

"How can that be managed?" asked Primus, Prime Minister Ashmore.

"They are gunning for war in the Ostmarkian court," said the foreign secretary. "The archduke is the sole dove in the cabinet, but he will not be able to outweigh the others."

"Yes, but having Ostmark and Illyria at war is not enough," said the Grand Master, shaking his head. "We need some means to bring Roxolana into conflict with Ostmark and then for Theudaland to enter the war in support of Ostmark."

"Grand Master," said Sword-bearer, War Minister Halberd. "And that's how it will be. As Gallia is attacked by Theudaland, we will nudge Roxolana to come into the conflict on the side of Gallia, with the help of the country's ambassadors here in Lynden, Bernhartdorf, and in Lutecia, Wolbozsky. Both of them are more in favor of the *Entente* than many nationals of Gallia and Pryden."

"Sequencing will be all-important," advised the Grand Master, Lord Edom. "And watch out for the doves in each government."

"Indeed, sir," replied the prime minister. "We will be sure to get it right. The key is the ruse to show that Pryden wants no war because she is bogged down in Eire with the rebellion. That will throw the Theudians off-balance, thinking we will not enter the fray and embolden them to attack Gallia. Were they to know we would enter, they might hesitate to take on both Gallia and Pryden. But Gallia alone they are confident of defeating."

"Well thought through," replied the Grand Master, "But thinking is not enough. This must be full-proof. We meet with the arms merchants tomorrow. We must have a fool-proof plan."

"It is fool-proof, Grand Master."

"It had better be."

▲ ▲ ▲

Imperial Palace, St. Paulusburg
July 1914

"The Ostmarkian army is massing on the border with Illyria supported by gunboats on the Danube. They now can shell the Illyrian capital, Plavigrad," reported Stolbetsin to the Tsar.

"The Ostmarkians have not declared war on Illyria yet, have they?"

"Not yet, but I fear they will do so soon if we do not defuse this situation."

"What do you recommend, Pavel Arsenievich?"

"Cables from your Majesty to the Theudian Kaiser and the Ostmarkian Emperor. Then, an immediate meeting of your Majesty with the Ostmarkian Emperor, the heir to the throne, and their foreign and war ministers."

"Where?"

"We will find a neutral venue but we must deal with the situation directly between our capitals. I am afraid that too much of Ostmark-Roxolan relations is in the hands of our respective envoys in the Illyrian capital, Plavigrad.

"Too many wars in the past have occurred because capitals relied on biased information from ambassadors who let their personal preferences influence the information that they sent home."

"They are good diplomats, Pavel Arsenievich, both our late Minister Hartmann and his counterpart, the Ostmarkian envoy, Minister Gierig."

"Good men, perhaps, Majesty, but diplomats with personal agendas that do not always coincide with the foreign policy goals of their capitals."

"So, what do you suggest?"

"We need more strategic diplomacy, Majesty. We need to bring your Majesty closer to the Ostmarkian emperor and I, too, must connect with the two prime ministers of their dual monarchy, the one for Ostmark and the one for Madjaria. The Ostmarkian prime minister, Karsten von Steyermark, is hawkish, but the level-headed Madjar minister-president, Count Imre von Patissus is keen to avoid war. I believe all of us in our respective capitals have been misled by our diplomats on the ground."

"Well, Hartmann is now dead."

"Yes, he suffered a massive heart attack while visiting the Ostmarkian envoy, Gierig, at their legation."

"Do you suspect foul play, as the Illyrian press claims, that Hartmann may have been poisoned in the legation or placed on a disguised electrified chair, whose current affected his heart?"

Stolbetsin shook his head. "Hartman was fat and had a weak heart. A heart attack was bound to happen. He liked high living and never dieted or took exercise."

"You say, both he and Gierig have done their capitals a disservice, as have the Ostmarkian ambassador here and our ambassador in Vedunia?"

"Yes, Hartmann was a Pan-Slavist, who stoked the fires of Greater Illyrianism, giving the Illyrians the impression that we here in St. Paulusburg supported the Illyrians' ambition to take over all of the Balkans, including the southern Slavic provinces of the Ostmarkian empire."

"What a loose cannon!" remarked the Tsar.

"Hartman also gave us the misleading impression," continued Stolbetsin, "that the Illyrians are accepted by the Latin Yeshuan Hrvatskis, the Orthodox Illyrian diaspora, and the *Yielder* Bassians, as the natural leaders of a south-Slavic state. That is a gross exaggeration. The majority of the Bassians of the *Yielder* faith and the Hrvatskis of the Latin Yeshuan faith do not want a Greater Illyria, or to be dominated by Orthodox Illyria. They do not wish to exchange one form of colonialism for another."

"Very interesting; I had always thought the southern Slavic idea very appealing."

"I'm afraid it is a romantic fiction, Majesty."

"Really?"

Stolbetsin nodded. "It is an idea best left to the poets. The fact is that the Hrvatski nationalists would prefer to have once again their kingdom as in the past or at least greater autonomy for their language, culture, and government, under the Ostmarkian empire, which, after all, shares a religion, culture, and history with them. Educated Hrvatskis look to Vedunia, not to Plavigrad, for their cultural cues. They see the Illyrians as semi-Orientals who have only recently emerged from the yoke of the Osmanli Turkic empire."

"I had not realized that."

"Yes, Majesty. The Hrvatskis do speak a South Slavic language that is very close to Illyrian, but they use the Latin script while the Illyrians use the Cyrillic script as we do in Roxolana. That makes a big difference for everything except colloquial interactions. An educated Hrvatski is more likely to choose a book to read in Theudian published in Vedunia than he is to read a book published in Plavigrad in Cyrillic script, which he would have to decipher, even if the underlying language is close to his mother tongue."

"What about the other side of the coin, the role of Minister Gierig, the Ostmarkian envoy in Plavigrad?"

"His name means 'greedy' in Theudian and other Germanic languages and you might say that he is stoking Ostmark's greed for the Balkans. He is playing to the military gallery that wants to annex Illyria as they annexed Bassia in 1908. Felix Friedmar, the heir to the throne, does not want that. Nor does Madjar Minister President Imre Patissus. But the generals do. We must work with and help Felix Friedmar and voices of reason like the prime minister of Madjaria.

"Indeed, Felix Friedmar seeks to pacify the Slavs by giving them equal voice to the Madjars in the empire, so that there will be a more stable three poles of power rather than the present two in the dual monarchy."

"Clever plan to empower the empire's Slavs. No wonder he had enemies at court with vested interests in the present dual monarchy who wanted him dead. What about the emperor's position?"

"The emperor is old and influenceable. He is close to his end and will probably die in the next couple of years. He is under the thumb of the military."

"So, the military must be frustrated that Felix Friedmar, their nominal head, was not killed in Saraybas."

"Indeed, I believe they were very much involved in the conspiracy to kill him, along with the Western bankers, and the arms dealers. At the very least, the military allowed the attack to occur by reducing the security around the archduke and widely publishing in advance the route that the motorcade would take on 28 June. Just by way of comparison, when the Ostmarkian emperor visited Saraybas in 1910, security was far tighter, with troops lining all the streets."

"So, do you think the military will try again to have the heir to throne killed?"

"I do not think so, Majesty. The archduke is being doubly careful now and has increased his security with officers and soldiers personally loyal to him. But I do believe that the military, the bankers, and the arms dealers have created a tidal wave of support for an invasion of Illyria and bent the ear of the emperor in that direction."

"We need to get through to them and undo the harm done by our envoys in Plavigrad."

"Yes, Majesty. Hartmann has died but Gierig is alive and well and stoking the fires of invasion. Another time, I will return to the question of our envoys in Lynden, Bernhartdorf, and our envoy in Lutecia, Wolbozsky. I believe they are playing a similar deceptive game as Hartmann and Gierig."

"There you go again about Wolbozsky and Bernhartdorf. You don't like those fellows, do you, Pavel Arsenievich?"

"My liking them or not is not the issue, Majesty. But Your Majesty has a right to honest, balanced information. I believe they are misleading you about Pryden and Gallia and doing everything to bring our country into a great war against the central powers."

"We will deal with Pryden and Gallia another time, Pavel Arsenievich. For now, let us focus on Ostmark-Madjaria."

"I will do your bidding, Majesty, and draft those cables for you."

▲▲▲

"What do you have for me, Pavel Arsenievich?"

"The entire layout of the Ostmarkian forces in their border province of Halichina, their strengths, weaknesses, and locations of their cannons."

"How did you manage to get them?"

"The Ostmarkian commander of the forces in Halichina — that

is Ostmarkian Piastya — happens to be a spy for us."

"Really? Amazing."

"The Ostmarkians do not know that, but they will be daunted if we use this knowledge in a negotiation with them over Illyria: in other words, should they annex Illyria, we would easily annex Halichina."

"But how do we keep the Theudians out of the conflict?"

"By not mobilizing on the frontier with East Prussau but only on the frontier with Ostmarkian Piastya or Halichina."

"Yes, I find it horrifying that the generals had told me earlier that partial mobilization was not possible because there was only a general mobilization plan, and you wisely made me break it up. So now, we can mobilize on the Ostmarkian border without mobilizing on the Theudaland border."

"I believe your Majesty has done the right thing by breaking up the mobilization plan into a partial and full."

"Why was there only a general mobilization plan in the past?"

"That is what our warmongers wanted, Majesty. I have since ensured that the partial mobilization plan has been properly prepared."

"Once again, you have my back, Pavel Arsenievich."

"At your service, Majesty, always."

▲ ▲ ▲

"Yes, Majesty. I think we have impressed on the Ostmarkians, finally, counteracting the spin of their envoy in the Illyrian capital that Roxolana is serious and will not tolerate an invasion of Illyria. This is not 1908 when we did not react to their annexation of Bassia-Herzogia, the former *Vilayet* of Bassia in the Osmanli Empire. They now understand that if they annex Illyria, we will easily annex Ostmarkian Piastya, Halichina. They were horrified to find out that we knew where their forces were located, but they don't know where ours are. We have the upper hand on the Ostmarkian border."

"Yes, your plan worked."

"Your plan, Majesty."

"You proposed it to me."

"But the decision was yours, Majesty."

"Colonel Gierig had truly given his capital the impression in their capital, Vedunia, that we in Roxolana would not react to an Ostmarkian invasion of Illyria, as we didn't in 1908 when they annexed the *Vilayet* of Bassia.

"Now they know that we would surely invade Ostmarkian Piastya, where they are weaker than we are. They would lose Ostmarkian Piastya even if they gain Illyria. I do not think they wish that at all."

"No, they do not."

"War between Roxolana and Ostmark-Madjaria has been averted for now, but the warmongers will start again."

The Tsar frowned. "How might they start?"

"The big business of war, Majesty, is a war between Gallia and Theudaland. It will be the bloodiest with the most munitions spent. I think that is where the war-mongers will now focus. It is going to be a great western war."

"But we are bound to Gallia by our alliance."

"It is a secret treaty that we can wriggle out of."

"We will lose national prestige and credibility."

"Not if we discourage war and they insist on it. I think they are pushing for war in Gallia to get back the territories of Elisaz and Lutringen. The Prydenians pretend they don't want war but they long for it. They feel Theudaland is too powerful, building up its navy and so on."

"So, you are saying Roxolana should keep out of the western conflict."

"Precisely, Majesty."

"I like your idea, Pavel Arsenievich."

"Our task now is to reassure the Kaiser that we want no war with him or with the other central powers, Ostmark-Madjaria or Latium."

The Tsar nodded. "Some Willy-Nicky correspondence in the Prydenian language is essential now."

"It is, Your Majesty."

"I want you to draft a cable to Willy from me."

"Right away, Majesty."

▲▲▲

"The results of your efforts have born fruit, Pavel Arsenievich," said the Tsar.

"Your efforts, Majesty. Your friendship with the other two emperors played an overwhelming part."

"As did your hard negotiations at ministerial level and the veiled threat of using our secret information on the Ostmark-Madjar positions in Halichina to win any conflict there with them."

"I think, Majesty, that it is time to launch the initiative of a new Three-Emperors-Alliance."

"A secret one?"

"Most definitely. At this complex time, with powers armed to the teeth, all secrecy is too little."

Bad Hohenburg, Theudaland
July 1914

"Nicky is too young to remember the earlier Three-Emperors-Alliance, the *Dreikaiserbund*, which his father, Tsar Andrei III, had signed," said the Kaiser at his resort of Bad Hohenburg in his fluent accentless Prydenian, acquired from his nanny and modernized by many vacations as a child with his royal Prydenian cousins, who were either descendants of Queen Vanessa of Pryden, 'the mother-in-law of Europe,' and her consort Prince Abelard, or descendants of the daughters of the king of Danerige, 'the father-in-law of Europe.'

"Of course, you and I, Freddy, were much younger."

Emperor Friedrich Johannes II of Ostmark-Madjaria nodded and said, "Pleasanter times. What a magnificent century our empires have enjoyed, Willy and Nicky, since the Congress of Vedunia in 1815 up to now. I feel that this marvelous century is about to end and we are going into something ghastly. I am not sure I want to live in this new century."

Tsar Nicanor II chimed in: "The century will be, Freddy and Willy, what we make of it. And the first step will be averting war, at least between the three of us."

While the three emperors were socializing and reminiscing about the magnificent century just gone by, their ministers were thrashing out the main points of the new, secret *Dreikaiserbund*. It provided for an agreement by which none of the three would attack nor participate in an alliance against the other. Each reserved the right to remain neutral in a conflict involving another of them and third parties.

Imperial Palace, St. Paulusburg
August 1914

Stolbetsin read the decoded cabled dispatches from the Roxolan ambassadors in Pryden and Gallia. A brutal war had erupted in the West, between Pryden, Gallia and Lotharia, on one side, and Theudaland and Ostmark-Madjaria on the other. He was relieved that Roxolana had savvily stayed out of it. Both warmongering ambassadors were frustrated that Roxolana had stayed neutral. Yet, he knew, they would be the first to ask for exemptions for their sons and peasants not to fight in the war, if Roxolana had gone for general mobilization. He did not know what to do with the two ambassadors. The Tsar protected them to the hilt. But to Stolbetsin they were both loose cannons.

Stolbetsin read Theudian, Ostmarkian, Gallic, and Prydenian newspapers and enjoyed comparing the lies that were told in each one. Even piecing together what was said would not bring one a single inch closer to the truth; the truth lay far afield. This war was not what the papers made it out to be. This was not a fight for justice. This was a scam to make money for arms manufacturers and bankers.

Imperial Palace, St. Paulusburg
May 1915

"The Westerners are playing dastardly games, Majesty."
"Where?"
"From our intelligence we have gathered that Pryden and Gallia

concluded on 26 April 1915, a secret 'Treaty of Lynden' with Latium, inducing the latter to discard the obligations of the Triple Alliance and to enter the war on the side of the Allies by the promise of territorial aggrandizement at Ostmark-Madjaria's expense.

"Latium was offered not only the Latin-populated Trentino and Trieste but also South Tirol, Gorizia, Istria, and northern Dalmatia. Soon, we expect that Latium will formally change sides and declare war on Ostmark-Madjaria. Our intelligence predicts it will occur soon, towards the end of this month."

"Well, we can't judge the Latins. We also changed sides, but formally are staying neutral."

"They all know that we are stronger than any invader. We dare them to try what Norbert Bonacasa attempted in 1812 and then to end up dying in the frosts of Roxolana."

8. A SIMMERING STEW

<u>Imperial Palace, St. Paulusburg</u>
<u>September 1916</u>

"There is, Your Majesty," said Stolbetsin, "a Roxolan stew simmering in Theudaland in a pot which will eventually be smuggled across the border and could boil over, burning all of us."

"What are you talking about, Pavel Arsenievich?" asked the Tsar.

"Revolution, Your Majesty."

"Tell me more about this potluck stew of revolution. Take your time, give me all the background."

"In the days of our forefathers, only people 'of good family' traveled to Theudaland to study or to see their royal or noble relatives. Now it is very different."

"How so?"

"Over the past decade and a half over three million people have emigrated from Roxolana, half of them Mazars."

"That's a good thing for Roxolana, isn't it? We would be better off if all the trouble-making Mazars left."

"Most of the Mazars, Your Majesty, have been emigrating to North Vespucia, which requires workers, but admits them only from Europe. They don't want immigrants of other races."

"But they don't mind Mazars?" said the Tsar, puzzled. "Do they consider those Tatar converts to Mazarism to be Europeans?"

"The North Vespucians take into account geographic origin. Since Roxolana is considered part of Europe, they allow in Roxolan Mazars."

"The North Vespucians don't seem to realize it, but they are making a big mistake. One day, they will regret it, for the Mazars will create havoc there as they have here and elsewhere, cheating, snatching, grabbing what they can, and then dominating their society."

"But our real problem, Majesty, is not with the Mazars who emigrate to North Vespucia but with those who go next door to

Theudaland. There is a large and growing community of Roxolan Mazars in Theudaland and Helvetia; and most, if not all, of them, are revolutionaries. They go there to study because of the quotas limiting admission of Mazars to our universities."

"I am surprised Willy has no quotas in his universities."

"There are also quotas for Mazars there and there is in their parliament talk of shrinking the quotas and blocking the immigration of Mazars, but that has yet to happen."

"We do have our extradition treaty with Theudaland for undesirables, anarchists, and others. We can bring them back in chains and put them in prison."

"But the treaty is rarely enforced and cumbersome to implement."

"What are these trouble-makers up to in Theudaland?"

"These revolutionaries publish journals," explained Stolbetsin, "which the Kaiser's police raid and close, but they then move to other cities, or to Helvetia. There, the lakeside city of Junipera has become a hotbed for Roxolan revolutionaries."

"Do you see these Mazar anarchists coming back to Roxolana?"

"Alas, I do, Majesty. I see them returning, funded by powerful patrons of their tribe from major Western capitals, particularly Lynden, New Lynden, Lutecia, Vedunia, and, of course, Berstadt."

"And their overall objective?"

"Overthrowing your government, Majesty, and installing a regime of terror, just like in Gallia in 1789."

"They seem to follow the same scenario, these revolutions."

"No wonder, Majesty; behind them are the same forces."

"Freemasons?"

"And other associated secret societies run by Mazar bankers and traders. No exception here."

"Their principles, if they have any?"

"They consider themselves enlightened, Majesty, and rational, so they want to do away with monarchy and religion."

"The two most important pillars of our society. What would be left but chaos?"

"Indeed, Majesty. They preach an egalitarian society without religion, led by workers and peasants."

"Someone would have to govern them. I cannot believe that they could consult all the workers all the time to govern."

"Indeed. A small clique of professional revolutionaries would lead and they would use all means available, including limitless violence, to govern and achieve their goals."

"That is clear enough from their terrorist acts. How many attempts on your life so far, Pavel Arsenievich?"

"Nineteen, Your Majesty."

"Imagine a government ruled that way."

"It would be ghastly indeed. What makes it easier for them is that they see themselves as a vanguard of insiders and treat the Roxolan people as outsiders."

"It begins with their religion and tribe, does it not? They consider themselves as the chosen ones and everyone else as 'the other nations.' So, it becomes easy for them to terrorize anyone who is not of their tribe. What do you propose we do to prevent the smuggling of this smelly simmering stew back into Roxolana?"

"A closer collaboration between the Kaiser's police and the *Okhrana*."

"I will certainly discuss it further with Willy, although he has bigger fish to fry, namely the war that Pryden and Gallia are waging against him."

▲ ▲ ▲

Peter and Paul Fortress, St. Paulusburg
January 1917

Stolbetsin looked at the wreck of a man before him, bloodied from extensive torture.

"This is the terrorist, Prime Minister," said the commander of the fortress, "who has provided us accurate information on the secret pathway that leads these rebels into Roxolana."

"Where is he from?"

"Yulissa city, sir."

"Hotbed of revolutionaries."

"He was a student in Theudaland for many years, joined a revolutionary group there, the Vozvushniks, then came back into our country a few months ago. He was denounced by a double agent of ours who had infiltrated the Vozvushniks. We arrested several of them, but this is the one with the most actionable information. He has told us all about two men that are of interest to you: Taraski and

Uralin."

"Oh, yes, those two."

"We have compiled a detailed report with as an annex the full transcript of our interrogation of him."

Stolbetsin looked out of the window for a moment, thinking of Taraski and Uralin and how to deal with them.

"What do we do with this fellow, Prime Minister?" said the commander.

"We respect rule of law, commandant. This is Roxolana. He will be tried by the special courts and then will be given what the revolutionaries now call the Stolbetsin necktie."

"Not hard labor in Severnia?"

The Prime Minister shook his head. "The Stolbetsin necktie. But only after due process, of course."

▲ ▲ ▲

Imperial Palace, St. Paulusburg
February 1917

"Majesty, I have the perfect solution to the problem of infiltration of revolutionaries and the low-level insurgency that we face, particularly in the west, in Borderland Province."

"Tell me, Pavel Arsenievich."

"An amnesty for the leaders of the revolution, particularly Uralin and Taraski."

"An amnesty? How would that help?"

"Let's take an analogy from gardening, Majesty. Assume you have weeds that have migrated to your neighbor's garden but have left seeds behind. You would like to recover cut weeds to serve as fertilizer so that the seeds in your garden sprout. Then, when the seeds germinate and come up, you mow them all down."

"You mean that bringing the amnestied leaders back will flush out a host of local supporters who can then be followed and brought to justice, as need be."

"Precisely, it is sometimes better to allow the enemy a chance to deploy, the better to then cut him down."

"A kind of convoluted logic, if I may say so, Pavel Arsenievich, but I see your point."

"It is bound to work."

"Would you publish a list of the amnestied revolutionaries in the papers?"

"Yes, Majesty, it would not be a general amnesty but one for the twenty or so worst of them, including Uralin and Tarasky, the greatest villains. Uralin is currently hiding out in Helvetia and Tarasky is in North Vespucia, under the tutelage of Mazar bankers."

"You would lure the two of them here, and once here, you would allow them some freedom to operate?"

"Yes, Majesty, and all the while infiltrating their Vozvushnik organization with double agents."

"I like it, Pavel Arsenievich. It is as clever as some of the tricks that the Mazar bankers play."

"With this difference, Majesty, that my tricks are in support of Mother Roxolana. The tricks of the Mazar bankers purport to destroy Mother Roxolana."

"You have my blessing to proceed, Pavel Arsenievich."

9. URALIN AND TARASKI

<u>Villa Bruna, Junipera, Helvetia,</u>
<u>March 1917</u>

Lord Edom looked at the small-statured bald man with a goatee that the financier and adventurer Adrian Paucus had just introduced to him. The bald man looked like a green-grocer or a pharmacist. "And this man will sow revolution in Roxolana?" he asked himself. The man's physique seemed very unlikely. Only the fellow's fiery eyes gave away the energy within him which was like that of a caged panther.

"Vassily Uralin," explained Adrian Paucus, "will be the revolutionary spearhead that we are all counting on — the point man of the vanguard of the proletariat."

"So, you are Uralin," said Lord Edom non-committally. "Tell me about the program you plan to launch in Roxolana."

"Lord Edom," replied Uralin, "we are seeking to mobilize workers and peasants and so our message will be, as you have instructed, very simple and threefold: peace, bread, and land. On my arrival in St. Paulusburg, my slogan, as agreed, will be 'all power to the *soviets*.'"

"Tell me more about these '*soviets*.'"

"Councils of workers and peasants, *milord*. They currently have no real power; they were underground but the amnesty and reprieve under Premier Stolbetsin now allow them to meet as they could not earlier. But they have no real power. These councils are talk-shops, window dressing that gives the impression of a more open, participative society. But real power rests fully with the cabinet, the Duma, and ultimately with the Tsar, with Stolbetsin pulling his strings."

"And with the tiny party you have over there, the Vozvushniks, how do you propose to give all power to these so-called *soviets*?"

"The masses are like a volcano, Lord Edom. One needs only to remove the hard lava top and the magma will flow forth."

"Nice geological metaphor, Uralin, but you face a police state. Stolbetsin has provided some space for these parties as a safety valve for the steam-engine of state. He is allowing a little steam to escape from the boiler. But Stolbetsin is not sharing any power. So, what does it mean to say, 'all power to the soviets?'"

"It may be a slogan for now, Lord Edom, but if we can uncap the volcano, the masses, like lava, will smother the Tsar, Stolbetsin, and the rest of the aristocracy of Roxolana, opening the way for a new regime."

"Describe the new regime that you foresee, Uralin."

"Lord Edom, in the Vozvushnik party I am surrounded by appeasers, most of them believe that the Vozvushniks can creep to power by collaborating with other groups. I do not. I believe that a massive revolution must be unleashed."

"Seems to me," said Lord Edom, enjoying, as usual, playing devil's advocate, "that you have a very hard sell. Pure revolution seems not on the minds of most of your so-called revolutionaries. Even the armchair revolutionaries do not want anyone but the landowners, that is the traditional aristocracy, bankers, and industrialists to wield power, but certainly not the workers, peasants, sailors, and soldiers. These revolutionary leaders fear rule by the masses. I have seen statements by some of your other party leaders. That's what they say – coalitions in the Duma and so on."

"That will have to change, Lord Edom, and I am the man to effect that change."

Lord Edom was beginning to like this unlikely revolutionary, this small-statured bald man with fiery eyes. "There are two important points that concern me, Uralin and I want to hear your intended actions on them."

"Yes, Lord Edom. Kindly tell me and I will address the points."

"First, what will you do for the Mazar community in Roxolana, and second, what will you do with the banking system if your Vozvushnik party comes to power."

Carefully briefed by Adrian Paucus on these two points, Uralin had come well prepared.

"Lord Edom," said Uralin, "I will make a public statement denouncing anti-Mazarism and *pogroms*. The entire platform of the Vozvushnik party is that the enemy is the capitalist but that the working people of all nationalities and faiths stand together, whether

Mazar, Orthodox Yeshuan, or Protestant."

Lord Edom nodded, "And what about banking?"

"I will announce that the Vozvushnik party will nationalize all banks into a single state bank, which will delink the *grivna* from gold and make it a debt-based currency, allowing for credit expansion. We will meet with the Edom Bank to launch a massive bond offering, something that Stolbetsin has avoided doing, so as not to be beholden to the international bankers, as he says."

"Even if he had," interrupted Lord Edom, "our bank would not have floated the bond offering for him because we do not like the Tsar's government."

Uralin nodded and continued, "When the Vozvushniks come to power, the Edom Bank will become the foreign correspondent bank of the state bank of Soviet Roxolana, once we establish the new regime. All foreign reserves of Soviet Roxolana will be held at the Edom Bank."

Lord Edom liked what he heard. "Very well, Uralin. You see to your next steps with Adrian Paucus here. He is making all the arrangements for your trip back to Roxolana, through Scandinavia and then Theudaland — no mean feat in wartime, but Paucus has contacts at the highest levels of the Kaiser's government and he will make it happen. Paucus is known as the man who makes the impossible happen."

Paucus beamed and bowed his head deferentially with gratitude to Lord Edom.

North Station, St. Paulusburg
April 16, 1917

On the train platform, a large crowd and a brass band awaited the balding man with a goatee. Newspapermen with cameras and flash equipment took pictures. The man poked his head out from the train, smiled, and waved his hat. The crowd cheered and began singing the socialist anthem, *Internationale*, and calling out, "Uralin! Uralin!"

"So that's the infamous Uralin," said Igor Andreich, an *Okhrana* agent, to his partner.

"Do we arrest him?"

Igor Andreich shook his head. "Our instructions are to follow him. We have double agents and informants inside the Vozvushnik party. We are to take action only when the time is ripe. That moment has not yet arrived. For now, let's just listen to him."

"What then, sir?"

"The Prime Minister's idea is 'to allow the weeds to sprout, to let the weeds flower,' and then for us 'to come and mow them down.' Otherwise, we cannot flush out the hidden seeds of those weeds. So, now the Tsar has provided this amnesty and these revolutionary leaders are back in the country. They will, without realizing it, help us root out all the hidden revolutionaries."

"Seems like a dangerous way to proceed, sir. This might provoke an avalanche. What if we can't stop the avalanche?"

Igor shook his head. "You are still young, Dmitri. Learn from the wiser and older people, like Stolbetsin. You need to let weeds flower first. Then you cut them down. Otherwise, they will remain underground and you never know how many there are or where they are."

"I guess that is wiser."

"It is."

▲ ▲ ▲

The balding man raised his hand to silence the crowd. He saw the Vozvushnik party leaders walking up to him, but he ignored them, turned to the crowd of workers and peasants, and said, "Comrades, working people of Roxolana, I bring you greetings from the International Socialist, and I hail you in your struggle against tyranny and oppression.

"On behalf of the Vozvushnik party, I bring you three messages: peace, bread, and land."

The crowd applauded and cried "Hurrah! Uralin! Uralin!"

Uralin raised his palm to stop the cheering and continued, "Peace means having the courage to resist the warmongers who would want Roxolana to break her neutrality and enter the predatory war of the capitalist imperialists. Foreign socialists are supporting the war, here the Vozvushniks will not.

"Bread means giving priority to food production over cash crops and guaranteeing a loaf per week for each family no matter what the conditions.

"Land means nationalizing all landholdings and transferring their ownership to the local councils of agricultural laborers and peasants.

"All banks in the country will be nationalized and united into a single national bank, to be controlled by the soviet of the workers' deputies."

"We must move from our constitutional monarchy to a republic of Soviets of the Deputies of Workers, Agricultural Laborers, and Peasants throughout the country, from top to bottom.

"We face many challenges. Roxolana must go through two stages of revolution. In the first stage, where we are now, power is vested in the bourgeoisie, represented by the current Duma. In the next stage, to which we aspire, power must be placed in the hands of the proletariat and the poorest sections of the peasants.

"We, the Vozvushniks, are a minority party but the path to power is not to form coalitions but to pass power directly to the soviets of workers and peasants, bypassing the present power structures of parliament.

"I call for an immediate congress of the Vozvushnik party. We must change our name to the Mordechist Party. I also call for a new movement, a new revolutionary International, which will connect workers and peasants in all countries, particularly those currently at war to show them that this is a war of the capitalists for which the workers pay in blood. Roxolana must continue to remain neutral and in other countries, all hostilities must stop."

"In the past, for just speaking one-tenth of what Uralin just said he would have been arrested and sent to the Peter and Paul Fortress to be tortured," noted Dmitri to Lieutenant Igor.

"Different times, different tactics, Dmitri. Live and learn."

"I don't understand, sir."

"Don't try to. Just do your job. Observe them and trust the policy we are following. We are merely widening our net. All these revolutionaries will eventually fall into it. Stolbetsin will tell us when."

▲▲▲

Edom Court, Lynden
April 1917

Lord Edom looked at the slight, unkempt man with wire-rimmed glasses and a goatee that Adrian Paucus had just introduced to him. The untidy man looked like a petty clerk or a bookkeeper. Edom wondered from where Adrian Paucus had dredged up these characters. First the green-grocer-like Uralin and now this badly-dressed Taraski in dire need of a haircut and beard trim. Non-assuming yes, but so unprepossessing. A revolutionary leader did not have to look like a great stage actor but why choose such an ugly fellow and one who looked so clearly a Mazar? Like Uralin, this second revolutionary leader had incandescent eyes. The power of these men seemed to reside in their hypnotic eyes — both of them. They seemed cut from the same cloth although they were different in their own ways.

"Lyubomir Taraski," said Adrian Paucus, "will be the international revolutionary that we are all counting on — the ambassador, of the vanguard of the proletariat. He will serve as the right-hand of Vassily Uralin and ensure liaison with the outside world."

"So, you are Taraski," said Lord Edom. "Tell me about the international side of the Vozvushnik program."

"International banking and trade will be fundamental to our planned new soviet society, Lord Edom, and I will ensure that the Edom and Gondol banks have privileged access to Roxolana, particularly to finance her trade. The Vozvushnik party will be the beachhead of the Edom and Gondol banks in Roxolana. Once we are in power, your access will be total."

"Remember not to limit that access to just the Edom and Gondol banks but to extend it to all members of our banking consortium, namely the Vogel bank in Lutecia, the Paucus bank in Berstadt, and the Safirberg bank in Vedunia. All of us have contributed to the costs of your mission, including the ten thousand *talents* that you are carrying in your suitcase. Never forget it, Taraski."

"I will not forget it, Lord Edom. You will always be able to count on me and while I cannot speak for Uralin, I know he would fully agree with me on this point."

"Good. Attend to the details of the next stage of your journey through Scandinavia and Theudaland with Adrian Paucus. You will follow in Uralin's footsteps and, as he did, make a nice splash on arrival in St. Paulusburg. Uralin and you must become the face of the Vozvushnik party, which you must have renamed as the Mordechist Party. Once in power, you will favor members of our tribe in senior appointments of your directorate, especially the secret police, and you shall all adopt party names to disguise your origins, just as you have done, Lazar Danilovich Schwarzstein."

"It shall be done, *milord.*"

"But don't count your chickens, Taraski. Seize power first."

▲ ▲ ▲

North Station, St. Paulusburg
4 May 1917

The slight-framed man emerging from the train, with his wire-rimmed glasses and a goatee beard, looked more like a Mazar used-clothes street hawker or a pawnshop owner than a revolutionary, thought the senior *Okhrana* officer watching the platform. The arrival of this second revolutionary, Lyub Taraski, was as noisy and tumultuous as that of Vassily Uralin a month earlier.

When the cheering died down, Tarasky said, "I have come to fight for the proletariat, the workers, who deserve power and freedom from oppression. A greater voice for workers and peasants!"

The *Okhrana* officer did not quite understand the Prime Minister's new policy. Anyone making a speech like this a few years ago would have been arrested on the spot, taken to the Peter and Paul Fortress, tortured, then dispatched to a labor camp in the snowy wastes of Severnia in the Far East of Roxolana. How was an individual allowed to deliver such speeches now? Where would this new freedom of speech lead? In any case, the Vozvushnik organization was now penetrated by moles and double agents, former detainees to whom the *Okhrana* had granted immunity from prosecution in exchange for actionable information.

Disguised as journalists and photographers, *Okhrana* agents were taking detailed notes and photographs of the crowd on the platform, particularly the most enthusiastic ones with placards and supportive body language. Soon, they would be reporting on the inner workings of the Vozvushniks, who had been allowed out of hiding into the open.

10. OCTOBER 1917

<u>Imperial Palace, St. Paulusburg</u>
<u>October 1917</u>

"The Vozvushniks are planning a coup," said Stolbetsin to the Tsar, "and it will be soon. Both Uralin and Taraski are now up and about and we shall be able to act."

"The weeds are ripe to be mowed down?"

"They are, Majesty."

"Now that Uralin and Taraski are both in Roxolana, do you believe that capturing them and the cronies around them in the Vozvushniks will put paid to the rebellion, the infiltration of mercenaries across the border from Theudaland?"

"They are the heads of the movement, Majesty. They have been lulled into complacency by the amnesty that you have given."

"What is their plan?"

"They are plotting what they call a 'color revolution,' named after a flower."

"A flower?"

"Yes, a 'chamomile' revolution."

"Chamomile, no less. Our national flower. They want to take possession of it."

"It's symbolic. They feel they can."

"And behind it are the Mazar financiers and the local Mazar terrorists."

"You know the old saying, Majesty."

"Yes, poor Mazars becomes terrorists, anarchists, and revolutionaries, while rich Mazars wage a financial war against Roxolana."

"Funny how skillful they are at infiltrating organizations, including the army and navy, and making propaganda to further their causes and fight our interests."

Edom Court, Lynden
November 1917

"The naive Roxolans thought they could avoid war by staying neutral and by aborting our October coup, arresting Uralin and Taraski and all the Vozvushnik leaders. The Tsar and Stolbetsin underestimated the other cards up our sleeve.

"Well, finally our revolutionaries are taking the fight to them by igniting a civil war," gloated Lord Edom in the chapel of Edom Court. He was dressed in his mask and robe as Grand Master of the Prydenian Pilgrims. "Tell me where we stand, Primus."

Primus, Prime Minister Sir Hubert Ashmore, took the floor. "We have been able to infiltrate revolutionary mercenaries, so-called international volunteers, from East Prussau into Roxolana, and attack police stations and barracks with bombs and gunfire. They are following guerrilla tactics but they are facing stiff resistance and retaliation from the Tsar's troops."

"Well, at least, there is fighting going on, shells and other munitions are being spent, and the Tsar is forced to buy more arms and ammunition from our companies," smiled Lord Edom. "Now, tell me, Primus, how things are going in the higher echelons of the Theudian government. How often is the Kaiser in touch with the Tsar?"

"In regular contact, sir, as befits cousins. Several cables per week."

"And the Tsar does not suspect that the revolutionary mercenaries enjoy government support in Theudaland?"

The Prime Minister shook his head. "No, Grand Master. But Globe-trotter can tell you more."

"Certainly, Primus," replied Globe-trotter, Foreign Minister Sir Edmund Graves. "The Kaiser has successfully distanced himself from the infiltration of revolutionaries across the border from his country into Roxolana and has even given the Tsar the impression that the Theudian police are cracking down on revolutionary cells in Theudaland that may be supplying the revolutionaries."

"Good," replied Lord Edom. "Remind me who our allies are in Theudaland."

"The military mostly," said War Minister Halberd, "plus the ubiquitous free-wheeling businessman, Adrian Paucus, who has secured most of the funding for the mercenaries from the banking and business community. The Theudian military does not trust Roxolana and fears a two-front war if Roxolana enters the war on the side of the Allies."

"Interesting logic," remarked Grand Master Lord Edom. "So, in the Theudians we have unlikely allies; the enemy of my enemy and so on."

"The Theudian military brass feel," continued War Minister Halberd, "that if Roxolana is occupied fighting a civil war, they would be less likely to enter the world war on the side of the Allies and take on Theudaland. And for Roxolana, it is much cheaper to fight a guerrilla war against Vozvushnik revolutionaries than to fight a conventional war against the central powers. So, absent any proof of Theudian military support for the mercenaries, the Roxolans will not confront Theudaland. And the Tsar and the Kaiser maintain their cozy relationship which helps smooth matters over."

"Very Germanic logic," said Lord Edom, nodding.

"At the same time," Foreign Minister Graves chimed in, "the Roxolans have not made the connection between the revolutionaries and outside powers to the point of wanting to declare war."

"This is a curious blind spot of the Roxolans," remarked Lord Edom.

"Indeed, Grand Master," added the foreign minister. "The foreign support has been disguised by the use of expatriates, Roxolan students in Theudaland. There is only one downside to this state of affairs."

"What is that?" asked Lord Edom.

"An increase in anti-Mazarism, both inside and outside Roxolana."

"How is that happening?"

"The revolutionaries who are caught are disproportionately of the Mazar community, and so 'revolutionary' and 'terrorist' have become synonymous with 'Mazar.'"

"In fact," added the war minister, "the slogans in Roxolana used by the Tsar's army is "Kill the Mazars; root out the revolutionaries; root out the traitors against Mother Roxolana."

Lord Edom let out a big laugh which perplexed the other four men. "You wonder why I am laughing?"

They nodded.

"This helps our cause for the national home for the Mazars in Falasteen. The more anti-Mazarism there is, the more emigration will take place, and we will ensure that these emigrants go straight to Falasteen leading to the eventual creation of Moledet."

"A kind of perverse logic, if I may say so, Grand Master," remarked the foreign minister, Sir Edward Graves.

Lord Edom glared at Graves through his mask and shook his head. "You people are so innocent."

They stared at him in stunned silence.

"Sometimes the shortest distance between two points is not a straight line but a jagged one. The route to the national home of my tribe will follow a very roundabout path with lots of bumps. Anti-Mazarism and *pogroms* are the inevitable bumps on the road to Moledet."

The four black-robed pilgrims shook their heads in disbelief at Lord Edom's reasoning.

"Remember what I have already said many times in our meetings. Everywhere, my tribe serves loyally the Prydenian empire. Many advances, particularly in southern Africa, have been possible only because of pioneers and investments supported by my tribe. Our man for Africa, Gnome-of-the-dark, will confirm that."

Gnome-of-the-dark, the adventurer Sir Arthur Milton, nodded. There was silence. The three others simply looked at Lord Edom.

The Grand Master continued, "But in return, I reiterate that my tribe wants its homeland. It is as simple as that. You, in the government, must bring that about, in parliament and the cabinet."

There was continued silence. The Grand Master looked at the foreign secretary and, after the man's clumsy remark about Edom's 'perverse logic,' he thought it was high time that Sir Edmund Graves were replaced by a man far more sympathetic to the Moledist cause and the interests of Edom's tribe, namely Sir Alfred Baltiford. Baltiford was a devout fundamentalist Yeshuan who believed implicitly that the second coming of Yeshua would only occur when the Mazar people were once more rulers in the Holy Land. And a shortcut to that goal would be to grant, from among the spoils of the great war that was raging in Western Europe and West Asia, the territory of Falasteen to the Mazar people as their national home, Moledet.

"Have we unleashed a whirlwind, Pavel Arsenievich?" asked the Tsar. "The slack we gave the revolutionaries has now sparked a civil war."

"The civil war was inevitable, Majesty. The terrorists are streaming in over the East Prussau border and Theudaland is too bogged down on the Western Front to stop the infiltration in the East; they are probably relieved the trouble-makers are leaving their territory. So, it is up to us to stop these Mazar anarchists using our Kozak cavalry and we are managing quite well."

"So, the heaviest fighting is in Borderland Province?"

"It is, Majesty, but it will not cross the Dnieper River."

"How can you be so certain?"

"They plan to make Borderland Province their stronghold, to establish what they call a 'soviet' — a council — there and use it as a base to attack the rest of our country."

"Dastardly, is it not?"

"Indeed, Majesty."

"I am concerned. We might have just continued with a repressive policy."

"It is sometimes better, Majesty, to drain an abscess than to let it fester. The abscess was in the Roxolan expatriate community in Theudaland, mostly Mazar, that was fomenting revolution. By allowing them to drain into our huge country, we can now follow them better and eliminate them. You see they grew in size over there. Over there we cannot destroy them legally. Once they cross the border, we can crush them without the trouble of extraditing them."

"Once again, Pavel Arsenievich, you outsmart even the Mazars!"

"Our ambassador in Lynden, Bernhartdorf, informs us that the Cabal may be turning its attention elsewhere. We may not face a lull in the civil war or the Cabal's support for it, but the banksters do seem to be opening up a new front for their activities, and this one is in West Asia. They are licking their chops to swallow a piece of the Osmanli empire as a homeland for the Mazars."

"Good," said the Tsar, "we could then send all our Mazars there."

Stolbetsin smiled. "Well, Majesty, believe it or not, that is exactly what the Cabal would want."

11. A NATIONAL HOME

<u>Lynden, November 1917</u>

Foreign Office
November 2nd, 1917

Dear Lord Edom,

I have much pleasure in conveying to you, on behalf of His Majesty's Government, the following declaration of sympathy with Mazar Moledist aspirations which has been submitted to, and approved by, the Cabinet.

'His Majesty's Government view with favor the establishment in Falasteen of a national home for the Mazar people, and will use their best endeavors to facilitate the achievement of this object, it being clearly understood that nothing shall be done which may prejudice the civil and religious rights of existing non-Mazar communities in Falasteen, or the rights and political status enjoyed by Mazars in any other country.'

I would be grateful if you would bring this declaration to the knowledge of the Moledist Federation.

Yours,

Alfred Baltiford

▲ ▲ ▲

"Congratulations, Lord Edom," said Jakob Gondol, the New Lynden financier. "You have done it. You have obtained from the foreign secretary what we might term the 'Baltiford Declaration', the letter that serves as marching orders for the Prydenian empire to deliver up a national home for our people."

"That's just the first step, Gondol," remarked Lord Edom. "We still have to await the end of this war and the carving up of the Osmanli empire, so that the Holy Land, the province of Falasteen, will come to us as our national home."

"So, Foreign Secretary Baltiford has sold the proverbial chickens before they have hatched, hasn't he?" said Salomon Safirberg with a smirk.

"Ah, but isn't it smart, Safirberg, to buy options and futures, especially when you know which way they will go?" said Edom with a smile. "I have just cornered the market for Falasteen."

"Well put, Edom, but now that you have the real estate, we need to populate it and with people of learning and substance, not some indigent ghetto-dwellers," said Safirberg.

"My thinking exactly and we need to plan," replied Edom.

"Mazars of substance will not want to leave the glittering cities of Europe to go and live in a swamp in West Asia," said Adrian Paucus.

"We'll have to drain the swamp first, won't we?" replied Nathan Vogel. "Both hydraulically and ethnically, ridding it of the Badawis."

"Yes," continued Paucus, "but just think about it, why would someone want to leave the great cities of Europe to go to Falasteen and live alongside hostile Badawi tribesmen, just so we might have a crusader fortress in the Near East to protect the Suez Canal, our oilfields, and other interests?".

"They will need incentives to emigrate, won't they?" said Gondol.

"More than incentives," said Edom, "they must feel *compelled* to emigrate, to make the definitive pilgrimage, or 'ascend' as we might call it, to the Holy Land."

"Compelled, you say, Edom?" asked Gondol.

"Yes, suppose, just suppose, that life for them in Europe were to become unbearable, or even worse, life-threatening; then, they would want to emigrate and 'ascend' to Moledet.

"That is the price of creating a nation, an ethnically pure Mazar nation," said Lord Edom. "We need Mazars of quality from Europe, people with capital, skills, and education, to construct a strong country, a Western outpost in a hostile region. I entertain ideas, gentlemen."

"Well, how about stoking the fires of anti-Mazarism in Europe?" suggested Gondol.

"Isn't that a bit cynical, Gondol?" asked Safirberg.

"I prefer to call it practical and effective," replied Gondol.

"Think of the treason trial of the Gallic officer, Captain Seitenfuss, a few years ago. A perfect example of blatant anti-Mazarism," remarked Vogel.

"Yes, well he was acquitted," observed Gondol.

"That's beside the point, Gondol," retorted Vogel. "Seitenfuss should not have been accused. He was assimilated, yet he was made a scapegoat."

"An isolated case," said Lord Edom. "The Mazar community in Gallia is well assimilated and prosperous. One of our secret societies engineered the Seitenfuss affair to unsettle these very comfortable Gallic Mazars, and make them consider, at least, emigration."

"What if you had a new legal code which actively discriminated against our tribe," suggested Gondol.

"Why would one want to change the legal code to something so dastardly?" replied Safirberg.

"It would flush our people out and force them to emigrate," said Lord Edom.

"Emigrate, yes, but why would they go to Falasteen?" asked Safirberg. "Would they not prefer North Vespucia?"

"There are immigration restrictions in North Vespucia," explained Gondol.

"We could ensure that there are restrictions elsewhere too, including here in Pryden," said Lord Edom. "We can make certain that parliaments tighten the entry restrictions further still."

"Seems Machiavellian, Lord Edom," complained Vogel.

"Merely breaking eggs to make omelets, gentlemen," said Lord Edom. "It is the only way. Life needs to become unbearable in Europe for Mazars so their only hope becomes migrating to Moledet, formerly Falasteen, since no one else will take them."

"But," objected Vogel, "Lord Edom, you propose only that the rich, educated, and able Mazars emigrate, but what about the poor, infirm, and unqualified ones after their life becomes impossible in Europe?"

Lord Edom gave a one-sided smile, "They are not our problem, Vogel. They would have to fend for themselves, wouldn't they, as Mazars have always done throughout history. No one did anything for the first Edoms in the Theudian ghetto. They pulled themselves up by their bootstraps."

"Yes, Lord Edom," insisted Vogel, "but if we are party to making life unbearable for them, don't we have a moral responsibility also to find a way out for them?"

Lord Edom shook his head, "Developing Moledet with qualified labor and ample capital comes first."

"Even above the lives of poor and vulnerable Mazars?"

"Even above them," said Lord Edom calmly.

"But just what kind of regime would reintroduce discriminatory laws against our people?" asked Safirberg. "It would set back the clock two hundred years, to before the time when, at the behest of the Illuminati, freemasons, and other secret societies, Emperor Norbert Bonacasa liberated the Mazars from the ghettos of Europe. Certainly not in a democratic society. Surely not in a post-monarchical republican Theudaland."

"No," said Lord Edom, "but a strongman coming to power, say in a vanquished, impoverished Theudaland would be able to introduce such legislation."

"A strongman?" asked Adrian Paucus.

"Yes," replied Lord Edom, "the Theudians deep down like strongmen."

"I agree," said Paucus. "Many will miss the Kaiser if he goes following the end of the war and a strongman will remind them of the Kaiser. They need that iron fist, either of the Kaiser or another iron chancellor."

"I would suggest he be a strongman from our kind," said Safirberg.

"Yes, but how would he overcome anti-Mazarism to reach power?" asked Vogel.

"Just as we are trying in Roxolana — through regime change, through a *coup d'état*," said Lord Edom.

"What about his popular appeal?" asked Gondol. "How would a Mazar appeal to the non-Mazar majority?"

"The majority will not know he is Mazar," explained Lord Edom.

"You are confusing me, Lord Edom," objected Vogel.

"Very simple actually," said Lord Edom. "We will use someone with partial Mazar ancestry but a typical Theudian surname, yet someone loyal to us. Then, we will groom him to become a strongman and head of state who serves our interests above all."

"The consensus in the *Entente*, after the war," explained Paucus, "seems to be to force the Kaiser to abdicate and then install a social-democratic republic."

"Yes, that is the plan," concurred Safirberg. "But how would you get our part-Mazar *Marrano*, if you will, into power and then make him into a strongman? It does not seem possible."

"Politics is the art of the possible, my friend," replied Lord Edom giving a one-sided smile.

"You sound like you have a candidate in mind, Lord Edom," remarked Vogel.

Edom nodded his head. "I do indeed. He is currently a soldier, and he will shortly become a minor hero. We are staging an opportunity for some heroics on the battlefield. We will get him decorated. He is a corporal."

"Is he one of us?" inquired Gondol. "A member of the tribe?"

Lord Edom nodded. "His biological maternal grandfather in Ostmark was my uncle, Moritz Westheimer," revealed Lord Edom. "His grandmother, Maria Elise, worked as a maidservant in my uncle's house, when she was sixteen years old. My uncle, an older man who liked young girls, took a shine to her and got her pregnant. Then my uncle married her off to a miller in her natal village and the child was raised as the miller's but my uncle always watched out for the young one, from a discreet distance, of course.

"Before my uncle died, he asked me to watch over the boy and any children of his. He left the boy a small inheritance which gave him a modicum of independence to study and live modestly. He acquired a basic education and became a petty functionary. When he died, that small inheritance passed on to his son who wanted to study art and architecture in Vedunia but didn't make it into the academy. When the war came, he enlisted as a Theudian. He is currently a corporal, as I said, on the Western front. After my uncle died, I took over oversight of his natural grandson's welfare."

"What do you plan to do with him?" asked Paucus.

"I will have him groomed to become," replied Lord Edom, "first a ruthless political fighter, then an elected member of parliament, and finally, Chancellor of Theudaland."

"Chancellor of Theudaland?" said Safirberg. "A mere corporal?"

"Yes," said Lord Edom, "he has the makings of a real tyrant."

"This is too far-fetched, Edom," said Gondol.

"Trust me, Gondol," replied Lord Edom. "This will work."

"What's the corporal's name, Lord Edom?" asked Vogel.

"Hayder," Edom replied, "Albrecht Hayder. Mark that name, it will become famous one day and will be on the lips of every Theudian, just as is the name of Kaiser today. They will hail him as the Germanic messiah. Theudians of all classes will cry, "Heil Hayder!" He will be a true son-of-a-bitch, but he will be *our* son-of-a-bitch, in dutiful service to *Ballum Gavor*."

"Now that we have dealt with," said Gondol, "the question of Moledet and the Theudian strongman who will help us send the useful Mazars there, we need to return to the question of reparations to impose on Theudaland."

"My bank has calculated the target figure of one hundred thousand tons of pure gold," said Lord Edom. "A nice round sum and an auspicious number according to the Mazar mystical texts. That's what we should set as the war reparations for Theudaland to pay. That's equivalent to 269 thousand million gold *thalers*."

"They will never be able to pay that much," said Gondol.

"Precisely," said Lord Edom, "but that's good. We want the Theudians perpetually enslaved by the reparations-debt. We can milk them dry by making them feel guilty. The yoke of such a huge debt will crush them, keep them vulnerable and poor, the better for us to use them through our strongman."

▲▲▲

Edom Court, Lynden
January 1918

"Welcome, Chelem Wuckerman," said Nissim Edom when the visitor had been shown into his study.

"Lord Edom," replied Wuckerman.

"All ready for Lutecia?"

"I am always preparing, *milord*, always."

"That's what sets us apart as a tribe, Wuckerman. We always go the extra mile, we persist, and we make it there. Now, what do you have for me?"

"A double agenda, *milord*. I know exactly what to say at the session that the big four are allowing us, under the chairmanship of the Gallic president, where I will speak of the national home for our people in Osmanli lands."

"Yes, but as you know that is just a starter. The Holy Land is still an Osmanli territory. We will have to await the San Remo conference and the coup de grace at Sevres, for the final disposition of the Osmanli Empire. In the meantime, keep inoculating the big four to the idea of Moledet. At least, the text of the Baltiford Declaration must find its way into the Verchamps Treaty. I am planning for the phrase 'Mazar state' to wind up in the treaty, rather than just 'national home.' Once that text is finalized, the actual decisions on the Holy Land will be taken at San Remo and Sevres."

"The Holy Land and Moledet are clear to me, *milord*, but what is less clear is what to do about Roxolana."

"Yes, Roxolana is proving to be a much harder nut to crack than I had thought."

"You are lacking Tchaikovsky's Nutcracker, *milord*."

Lord Edom chuckled. "You, Wuckerman, will have to bring me a nutcracker from Roxolana!"

"Seriously, *milord*, I am searching for the right formula to bring the rebels and the government from Roxolana together during the Lutecia peace conference."

"Yes, the Tsar has been refusing all offers to negotiate with our rebels, our revolutionaries."

"I think there is some resentment in the West that Roxolana did not abide by the *Entente* and come into the fray."

"The Roxolans were smart; they preserved their population and infrastructure. In some ways, I admit, smarter than we bankers were in fomenting the rebellion. We still have not been able to do away with their gold-based currency and introduce a debt-based currency that we can manipulate at ease."

"It's that Stolbetsin, *milord*. He has the Tsar's ear."

"More than that, Wuckerman, Stolbetsin runs the show. He is another 'iron chancellor,' like Biesemereg of Theudaland. The Tsar spouts forth what Stolbetsin tells him to say, especially in foreign affairs matters."

"Well," said Wuckerman, "Roxolana has an observer at the Lutecia peace conference, the former foreign minister and the brother-in-law of Stolbetsin, namely Samsonov."

"You must get close to him, Wuckerman."

"I will, *milord*."

"More importantly, Wuckerman, you must invite them to a lavish dinner. I will have a Gallic businessman from our tribe lend you his five-hundred square meter apartment on the Avenue Montaigne and you show them a good time, bring together the rebels and Samsonov and his delegation. There should be some traction there."

"Sounds good, *milord*."

"Then come back."

"Other instructions, *milord*?"

"Yes, you must help me with my disinformation, to keep the Edom name far from the agenda of Roxolana and the Holy Land."

"Whatever you want, *milord*."

"Well, I will ask my Gallic cousin, Evariste Edom, to send an anti-Moledist journalist openly backed by him to criticize the Baltiford Declaration. It will help distance the Edom family from the initiative. We don't want it to be seen for what it is, an Edom initiative. For that purpose, I want his journalist to come and give a speech against the Baltiford Declaration. It will sound like the Edom family opposes the Baltiford Declaration and the idea of a national home. Even though the declaration is addressed to us. So, it will also gain us some favor with the Badawi delegation of Emir Faddoul. You must also get close to the Badawis."

"Will do, *milord*."

Temple Hope, Lynden
February 1918

"Allow me to introduce to the congregation, Dr. Chelem Wuckerman, an esteemed chemist with several patents to his name, and most recently, the champion of Moledet, the proposed national home of our people in Falasteen, West Asia."

Dr. Wuckerman had been invited to speak on the proposal for Moledet at Temple Hope, one of the largest Mazar congregations in Lynden. He made his case for Moledet. There were few questions. Then unexpectedly for Wuckerman, his host, the master, or pastor, of the congregation, Master Emile Eidelberg, began to argue with him.

"Dr. Wuckerman, I am afraid that this idea of Moledet is misplaced. Our people are in the diaspora because that was God's will. One day, when the Messiah comes, he will lead all our people back to the Holy Land. In the meantime, we must live our lives honestly in the diaspora."

"That will not work," said Wuckerman. "All of you just don't get it. The only place for the Mazars is in Moledet. It will be the Mazar nation."

"It seems to me, Dr. Wuckerman, that you are confusing religion with nationality. We are above all here in the diaspora loyal nationals of the countries where we live but practice our religion freely in private. There is no contradiction between our civic life as Prydenians and our religious life as Mazars. We see no reason to leave all of this and go to the desert of Falasteen."

"You are lucky. For now, you are safe, but look at what happened to Captain Seitenfuss in Gallia."

"An isolated case. And some say that the case was staged to create the impression of anti-Mazarism. The Mazar people in Gallia are a prosperous happy community."

"Was it an isolated case? Was it a stage-managed incident? Then, consider the *pogroms* in the Roxolan Empire."

"That is a less civilized East European state. Our reality in Pryden is different and much more pleasant."

"But there are over five million members of our tribe in the Roxolan Empire. They will be happier in Moledet, their own country, instead of being second-class citizens in Roxolana."

"I disagree. The solution is for them to lead good Mazar lives and abide by the Tsar's laws. In time, God will improve their conditions. Their circumstances have already improved greatly since the time of Queen Xenia the Great."

"Master, you have lived and grown up in Pryden, where you enjoy all the civil liberties. Think of our poor brethren under the Tsar's despotism."

"We have had despotism here in Pryden. We were expelled from Pryden in the thirteenth century and then only allowed back in the seventeenth century. Restrictions are part of the diaspora, but they have not prevented our community from prospering here in Pryden. Slowly, we have gained prominence. We have even had a Mazar prime minister. But that is not the point. The point is that we can practice our faith here freely and make an honest living."

"You are missing the point and holding back five million oppressed Mazars in Roxolana by not supporting Moledet."

"You will find, Dr. Wuckerman, very little support in this congregation for Moledet." He turned to the congregation. "A show of hands, please. Who here would like to pack up and leave Pryden for the desert of Falasteen to build a new country just for the Mazars?"

No one raised their hands.

"You see?" said the Master.

Dr. Wuckerman shook his head. "You people are all mistaken. You cannot see the writing on the wall."

"No, Dr. Wuckerman, it is you who are mistaken. This idea of Moledet will bring our people no peace. You are seeking to create a territorial ghetto in a hostile region when we have finally emerged from the ghettos of Europe."

"Except in Roxolana."

"Excuse me, Dr. Wuckerman, I have traveled in Roxolana. Increasingly, they are leaving the Settlement Area for the big cities. In time, they will gain all the rights of Roxolan citizens."

"Wishful thinking."

"Yours is wishful thinking," argued the Master back. "You will find few takers for Moledet, as you saw from the show of hands."

"Maybe not here in your comfortable congregation," said Dr. Wuckerman, "But in the East, certainly."

"Not in Gallia, not in Theudaland, nor in Lotharia…"

Dr. Wuckerman took leave of the congregation and left in a bitter mood.

12. THE PEACE TREATY

Lutecia, Gallia, 1919

In the protracted negotiations of the peace treaty in Lutecia, the capital of Gallia, following the November 1918 armistice between the Allies and the Central Powers, the Edoms were nowhere to be seen, but they were secretly represented through their agents. Each of the big four Allied victors, the heads of state or government of North Vespucia, Pryden, Gallia, and Latium had assistants and advisers who could be traced back to Lord Edom, either directly or through proxies, and whose agenda they quietly promoted in their daily meetings at 6 pm when their principals had retired for the evening to prepare for dinner and socializing. At these closed-door evening meetings, the sherpas would plan the next day as they pored over maps with red pencils, compasses, and rulers to divide up the three vanquished empires. These men were the driving force behind the conference and the men who had crossed the i's and dotted the t's. These advisers understood geography and geopolitics. The heads of state and government did not.

▲ ▲ ▲

Gallic Foreign Ministry,
Quai de la Grenouillère, Lutecia
6 February 1919

In his flowing robes, Emir Faddoul of Badawia, a hereditary ruler whom the Prydenians had backed in a rebellion against the Osmanli overlords, took the floor at the Lutecia peace conference and delivered in the Badawi language a speech that had been prepared for him by his close adviser, Colonel T.E. Lawford, who had fought by his side during his successful revolt against the Osmanlis:

"Excellencies, the country from the Mediterranean Sea southward to the Meluccan Ocean is inhabited by 'Badawis' – by which we mean people of closely related stocks, all speaking the one language, Badawi. The non-Badawi-speaking elements in this area do not, I believe, exceed one percent of the whole.

"The Badawi nationalist movements seek to unite the Badawis eventually into one nation. I commanded the Assyrian Revolt and had under me Assyrians, Mesopotamians, and nomadic Badawis.

"We believe that our ideal of Badawi unity in West Asia is justified beyond any need of argument. If an argument is required, we would point to the general principles accepted by the allies when the Republic of North Vespucia joined them, to our splendid past, to the tenacity with which our race has for six hundred years resisted Osmanli attempts to absorb us, and, in a lesser degree, to what we tried our best to do in this war as one of the allies.

"My father has a privileged place among the Badawis, as their successful leader, and as the head of their greatest family, and as Sheriff of Mehrab, the holiest city of our *Yielder* religion. He is convinced of the ultimate triumph of the ideal of unity, if no attempt is made now to force it, by imposing an artificial political unity on the whole or to hinder it, by dividing the area as spoils of war among great powers.

"The unity of the Badawis in West Asia has been facilitated by the development of railways, telegraphs, and airways. In the olden days, the area was too huge, and in parts necessarily too thinly peopled, to communicate common ideas readily.

"The various provinces of Badawi Asia – Assyria, Uruk, Jezireh, Hejaz, Nejd, and Yemen – are very different economically and socially, and it is impossible to constrain them into one frame of government.

"We believe that Assyria is sufficiently advanced politically to manage her internal affairs. We feel also that foreign technical advice and help will be a valuable factor in our national growth. We are willing to pay for this help in cash; we cannot sacrifice for it any part of the freedom we have just won for ourselves by force of arms.

"Jezireh and Uruk are two huge provinces, made up of three civilized towns, divided by large wastes thinly peopled by semi-nomadic tribes. The world wishes to exploit Mesopotamia rapidly, and we, therefore, believe that the system of government there will have to be buttressed by the men and material resources of a great foreign power.

"We ask, however, that the government be Badawi, in principle and spirit, the selective rather than the elective principle being necessarily followed in the neglected districts until time makes the broader basis possible. The main duty of the Badawi government there would be to oversee the educational processes which are to advance the tribes to the moral level of the towns.

"The Hejaz is mainly a tribal area, and the government will remain, as in the past, suited to patriarchal conditions. We appreciate these better than Europe and propose therefore to retain our complete independence there.

"The Yemen and Nejd are not likely to submit their cases to the Peace Conference. They look after themselves, and adjust their relations with the Hejaz and elsewhere.

"In Falasteen, the enormous majority of the people are Badawis. The Mazars are very close to the Badawis in blood, and there is no conflict of character between the two races. In principle, we are absolutely at one. Nevertheless, the Badawis cannot risk assuming the responsibility of holding level the scales in the clash of races and religions that have, in this one province, so often involved the world in difficulties. They would wish for the oversight of a great trustee, so long as a representative local administration commended itself by actively promoting the material prosperity of the country.

"In discussing our provinces in detail, I do not lay claim to superior competence. The powers will, I hope, find better means to give fuller effect to the aims of our national movement. I came to Europe, on behalf of my father and the Badawis of West Asia, to say that they are expecting the powers at the Conference not to attach undue importance to superficial differences of condition, and not to consider them only from the low ground of existing European material interests and supposed spheres. They expect the powers to think of them as one potential people, jealous of their language and liberty, and ask that no step be taken inconsistent with the prospect of an eventual union of these areas under one sovereign government.

"In laying stress on the difference in the social condition of our provinces, I do not wish to give the impression that there exists any real conflict of ideals, material interests, creeds, or character rendering our union impossible. The greatest obstacle we have to overcome is local ignorance, for which the Osmanli Government is largely responsible.

"In our opinion, if our independence be conceded and our local competence established, the natural influences of race, language, and interest will soon draw us together into one people; but for this, the Great Powers will have to ensure us open internal frontiers, common railways and telegraphs, and uniform systems of education. To achieve this, they must lay aside the thought of individual profits and their old jealousies. In brief, we ask you not to force your whole civilization upon us, but to help us to pick out what serves us from your experience. In return, we can offer you little but gratitude."

▲ ▲ ▲

Gallic Foreign Ministry,
Quai de la Grenouillère, Lutecia
12 February 1919

Chelem Wuckerman took the floor before the assembled delegates and made the case for the national home for his people. His speech had been prepared by many hands in the Moledist organization and had been approved by Lord Edom:

"Distinguished delegates, the claims of the Mazars concerning Falasteen rest upon the following main considerations:

"First, this land is the historic home of the Mazars; there they achieved their greatest development; from the center, through their agency, there emanated spiritual and moral influences of supreme value to mankind. By violence, they were driven from Falasteen, and through the ages, they have never ceased to cherish the longing and the hope of a return.

"Second, in some parts of the world, and particularly in Eastern Europe, the conditions of life of millions of Mazars are deplorable. Forming often a congested population, denied the opportunities which would make a healthy development possible, the need for fresh outlets is urgent, both for their own sake and the interests of the population of other races, among whom they dwell. Falasteen would offer one such outlet. To the Mazar masses, it is the country above all others in which they would most wish to cast their lot. By the methods of economic development to which we shall refer later,

Falasteen can be made now, as it was in ancient times, the home of a prosperous population many times as numerous as that which now inhabits it.

"Third, Falasteen is not large enough to contain more than a proportion of the Mazars of the world. The greater part of the fourteen million or more scattered throughout all countries must remain in their present localities, and it will doubtless be one of the cares of the Peace Conference to ensnare for them, wherever they have been oppressed, as for all peoples, equal rights, and humane conditions. A Mazar National Home in Falasteen will, however, be of high value to them also. Its influence will permeate the Mazaries of the world, it will inspire these millions, hitherto often despairing, with new hope; it will hold out before their eyes a higher standard; it will help to make them even more useful citizens in the lands in which they dwell.

"Fourth, such a Falasteen would be of value also to the world at large, whose real wealth consists in the healthy diversities of its civilizations.

"Finally, the land itself needs redemption. Much of it is left desolate. Its present condition is a standing reproach. Two things are necessary for that redemption -- a stable and enlightened Government, and an addition to the present population which shall be energetic, intelligent, devoted to the country, and backed by the large financial resources that are indispensable for development. Such a population the Mazars alone can supply.

"Inspired by these ideas, Mazar activities, particularly during the last thirty years, have been directed to Falasteen within the measure that the Osmanli administrative system allowed. Millions of pounds sterling have been spent in the country, particularly in the foundation of agricultural settlements. These settlements have been, for the most part, highly successful.

"With enterprise and skill, the Mazars have adopted modern scientific methods and have shown themselves to be capable agriculturalists. The ancient Mazar tongue has been revived as a living language; it is the medium of instruction in the schools and the tongue is in daily use among the rising generation. The foundations of a Mazar University have been laid at Urshalim and considerable funds have been contributed for the creation of its building and its endowment.

"Since the Prydenian occupation, the Moledist Organization has expended in Falasteen approximately 50,000 Prydenian *libras* a month upon relief, education, and sanitation. To promote the future development of the country, great sums will be needed for drainage, irrigation, roads, railways, harbors, and public works of all kinds, as well as for land settlement and house building. Assuming a political settlement under which the establishment of a Mazar national home in Falasteen is assured, the Mazars of the world will make every effort to provide the vast sums of money that will be needed.

"Hundreds of thousands of Mazars pray for the opportunity speedily to begin life anew in Falasteen. Messengers have gone out from many places, and groups of young Mazar men proceeding on foot have already reached Trieste and Latium on their weary pilgrimage to Moledet."

▲ ▲ ▲

"Colonel T.E. Lawford is a thorn in our side," railed Chelem Wuckerman in a meeting at Edom Court with Lord Edom and Sir Alexander Witzel of the Pryden-Melucca Office, which was responsible for all Prydenian policy matters related to West and South Asia, including Falasteen. "He is pumping up that towel-head Emir Faddoul that the Prydenian government have dredged up in the Hedjaz and are trying to present as king of all the Badawis."

"Now, now, Wuckerman, calm down," said Lord Edom, "Easy does it. We have all the cards in our hand."

"Lord Edom," replied Wuckerman, "did you read that statement the emir delivered on 6 February in Lutecia, which was written for him by Colonel T.E. Lawford? He wants all the Badawi lands between the Mediterranean Sea and the Meluccan Ocean, including Falasteen, the land for our future national home."

"Yes, of course, and I understand you have met with the emir since then and agreed on a two-state solution."

"Yes, but without Colonel Lawford, the emir is nothing, he is lost. He would still be riding a camel in the desert. Now he wants all of Assyria, Mesopotamia, the Badawi Peninsula, and Falasteen!"

Lord Edom was enjoying playing devil's advocate. "But he did say, Wuckerman, did he not, that the Mazars and Badawis are of common blood, and in principle have no conflict?"

"He did, but his speech at the peace conference, *milord*, calls for a Badawi government in all those regions, including Falasteen, our future Moledet. Only one community can have sovereignty there. It is either they or we."

"What about the two states you both talked about?" asked Edom.

"It was a mere face-saving device for both of us, *milord*. You know that we Moledists have clearly declared our expected frontiers: from the Mediterranean shore in the east to the edge of Mesopotamia in the west, up north to the hills of Lubnan, and down south to the Gulf of Ayla. Our request to the peace conference is for all of that area."

"All of it? Do we need all of it? As a base, as an outpost to defend Prydenian regional strategic interests, wouldn't just the land between the Mediterranean Sea and the Urdun River be enough?"

"Lord Edom, Colonel Lawford must go!" said Wuckerman, raising his voice to bring the discussion back to what was bothering him. "He is the one putting these extravagant ideas in the Emir's head. Before Lawford, the Emir barely knew his desert neighborhood and had few ambitions beyond that."

Ignoring Wuckerman's excitement, Edom turned to Sir Alexander, who had remained quiet. "What do you think, Witzel?"

"Wuckerman is right, *milord*. Colonel Lawford is indeed dangerous for our cause. He is intelligent, well-educated, articulate, and influential. He is the hero of the victory over the Osmanlis. He has Emir Faddoul eating out of his hand and he talks back even to our sovereign."

"Indeed, Witzel? This I want to hear."

"Yes, sir. After his adventures leading the Badawi revolt to defeat the Osmanlis, Lawford was summoned before His Majesty here in Lynden."

"And?"

"The sovereign wanted to decorate Lawford with a medal. Do you know what the colonel did?"

Edom said, raising his eyebrows, "Tell me, Witzel."

"Lawford refused the king's medal."

"Did he now?" said Edom, grinning. "I am beginning to like this fellow!"

"Don't you want to know the reason why?"

Edom shook his head, "It doesn't matter, Witzel. Lawford is not going to hinder our plans."

"Lawford said, 'Your Majesty, in all conscience, I cannot accept your medal because I feel ashamed of how our government has let down the Badawis by promising them sovereignty and then recolonizing them jointly with the Gallics, based on the secret Syburn-Poirot agreement to divide up the Near East.'"

Lord Edom grinned. "Good for him! The man has character. I might almost say he was a Mazar. He certainly has *chutzpah* — pluck. Has he no Mazar blood?"

"He does not, *milord*, but what I am talking about is serious," objected Wuckerman. "At the Lutecia conference, Lawford spent much time with the famous media man from North Vespucia, Lowden Thorpe, who wrote a widely-read article on him. Soon, Lawford's point of view on the Falasteen question and the Badawi claims to the region will become public knowledge and would sway opinion against the Moledist cause."

"Lowden Thorpe, you say?" asked Lord Edom. "I have heard that name before."

"Yes, sir. He is a larger-than-life North Vespucian journalist, writer, and film-maker. Very influential. He traveled to the Badawi lands, befriended Lawford, and is making him famous along with Emir Faddoul. The romanticism of the Badawi cause, with the camels, the sands, and so on is swaying public opinion in favor of them in both Pryden and North Vespucia as well as in Gallia.

"I am afraid, Lord Edom, that the Baltiford Declaration, the statement of the Gallic foreign ministry in favor of a Mazar national home, and even any favorable language we might expect in the final peace treaty, quoting these documents, will mean nothing in the court of public opinion, where the likes of Colonel Lawford, Lowden Thorpe, and Emir Faddoul will carry the day. The public will espouse the Badawi cause. And in contrast, the Mazars are generally hated, seen as money-lenders, petty shopkeepers who cheat customers, and so on. There will be little public sympathy for them to be given a national home."

"What would you have us do with Colonel Lawford?" asked Lord Edom.

"He needs to suffer an accident, *milord*. One word from you to the right people and His Majesty's secret services will take care of it."

"Really now, Wuckerman and Witzel, you can't be serious? Bump off Colonel Lawford? The famous Lawford of Badawia?"

"Dead serious, *milord*," replied Witzel.

Wuckerman nodded, too. "Witzel is taking no chances. We cannot afford to. The Moledist cause cannot be put at risk."

"That colonel in a Badawi headdress will soon fade from the scene," chuckled Lord Edom. "The post-war world has other pressing matters to attend to than the fate of the Badawis."

"Can you run the risk that he will not fade away, *milord*?"

"Very well then, gentlemen, I'll put in the right word."

"One word, *milord*," said Witzel, "just one word from you, that's all it takes. That word will trickle down the food chain and the secret services will spring into action, as they always have."

▲ ▲ ▲

It was Sunday morning and it was pouring with rain in Kewford, to where Lawford had returned from the Lutecia peace conference to visit his ailing father. Having braved sandstorms, blizzards, and tropical rains on his many travels across the world, Lawford was not one to be daunted by the elements, and particularly not by Prydenian rainfall no matter how heavy.

He put on his leather cap, more to keep his hair dry and the wind out of his ears than to offer any crash protection, adjusted his goggles, and eased his motorcycle out of his garage, and started it up.

The machine was a 1916 Brough flat-twin of 6 hp rating, with a 70mm bore and 90mm stroke, displacing 692cc. Proud of his powerful wartime motorbike, Lawford had nicknamed it "Bar," short for "Bar-regesh" or "Son of Thunder" in Aramaic.

Lawford turned off his side road onto the main thoroughfare and began to gather speed. There was a dip in the road that he was used to but which reduced his visibility. He coasted into the depression without accelerating further.

As he came up out of the dip, he saw two cyclists ahead of him, pedaling in a bizarre zig-zag pattern so that they blocked the road entirely. He swerved to avoid them. The motorcycle skidded off the road and hit some rocks. Lawford was thrown clear of the machine and hit his head on a tree.

▲ ▲ ▲

The cyclists dismounted and came up to the wreckage to examine the body.

"He is out cold but still breathing," said the shorter man to the taller one.

"We'll soon take care of that," replied the latter.

The taller man withdrew from an inner pocket of his leather jacket a metal box and opened it, and withdrew a syringe. He inserted the needle into Lawford's neck and released the contents of the syringe into the colonel's bloodstream. Lawford soon stopped breathing.

The man put the syringe away and checked Lawford's wrist. Finding no pulse, he said "Righto," and nodded to his companion. "Undetectable substance. Will look like he died from his injuries."

The two men mounted their bicycles and pedaled calmly away in the rain, leaving the motorcycle wreck and Lawford's corpse behind them.

▲ ▲ ▲

Across the world, people mourned "Lawford of Badawia," and the New Lynden Times in North Vespucia termed it a "tragic waste" and suggested that the road incident that had caused Lawford's demise was "unwarranted and perhaps avoidable."

No one mourned Colonel T.E. Lawford more than Emir Faddoul. With his sherpa and protector gone, the Badawi leader felt exposed and abandoned. He returned home to Assyria to discover that the Prydenian army, which had conquered the former Osmanli province along with him, was packing up to leave, as per the peace treaty.

Ignored by the Lutecia peace conference and with his nationalist aspirations left out of the final treaty, Emir Faddoul simply declared himself ruler of Assyria and all the Badawi lands from the Mediterranean to the Meluccan Ocean. However, the Gallic army soon arrived in Assyria to relieve the Prydenians, as per the once-secret Syburn-Poirot agreement to divide up the Near East, which was now incorporated into the peace treaty that had emerged from the Lutecia conference. Shortly thereafter, Emir Faddoul was forced to flee Assyria and sought asylum in Latium.

The Mazar tribe and the Moledists hailed the mandate that had been given under the treaty to Pryden to administer Falasteen — the Holy Land of the Good Book — for they trusted the Prydenians more than they did the Gallics, whom they saw, despite their declarations in favor of Moledet, as essentially pro-Badawi and anti-Moledist. The Gallics had many colonies in Badawi lands in North Africa and now in West Asia and they were not interested in stirring up unrest among their subject Badawi populations by overtly supporting the Moledet cause.

Verchamps Palace, 28 June 1919

One by one the delegations came to sign the treaty before them in the glittering Hall of Mirrors in the Verchamps Palace. The Theudian delegates had tears in their eyes. The symbology of the event had been designed to humiliate the Theudians. The date set was the fifth anniversary of the attempt that had been made on the archduke's life. In this very hall, after the capitulation of Gallic forces to Prussau's army in the Gallia-Prussau war, the Theudian Empire had been declared in 1871 when the King of Prussau had become the Emperor of Theudaland. Now, almost half a century later, the Gallic president smirked under his walrus mustache, savoring sweet revenge. Little did he know that this would not be the last time revenge would be savored in this hall.

13. BETTER DAYS AHEAD

Mönchenstadt, Theudaland
October 1932

The courtyard had known better days. It was walled in on all sides by tenement buildings with an access gate to the street that remained open, allowing stray dogs and cats to wander in and out to forage in the garbage overflowing from bins by each of the building entrances. Garbage collection was irregular, as the city sanitation crews had not been paid in weeks. The city was in the throes of a deep recession.

The great crash of 1929 had begun in the financial district of New Lynden in North Vespucia but had caused an economic depression that had now spread all over the world and had hit Theudaland and its people particularly hard. With the rampant hyperinflation, it now took a barrow-full of *thaler* notes to buy a loaf of bread, when bread was available. Meanwhile, the bankers in Theudaland, North Vespucia, Pryden, and other countries who had foreseen the crash had sold securities short and were now buying up real and financial assets at a fraction of the high values they had reached before the crash.

From several of the windows hung tattered laundry spread out to dry on thin clotheslines with wooden cloth pegs. In one corner of a courtyard was a small bonfire over which a group of children was roasting on spits the carcasses of a dog and a cat. The skins of the animals lay in a pile of trash in another corner. The children, dressed in rags, were thin, most of them with their ribs showing. A teenage girl held a small hungry baby which was crying at the top of its lungs.

On a doorstep, in another part of the courtyard, watching the children, sat two unshaven war veterans, one of whom had lost his left leg below the knee from shrapnel, and the other his right eye from a bullet wound.

Pointing to the children, the one-eyed veteran said, "That is what happens when you lose a war, Werner."

"No, Hans," replied his companion, "that's what happens when banksters and politicians sell your country down the river."

"You mean, the Verchamps Treaty?"

"The Verchamps *Diktat*! That accursed document *dictated* misery and suffering on our country."

"Our country was sold for peanuts to the Mazar banksters."

"Imagine, a guilt clause that placed the entire blame for the war on Theudaland and its allies and demanded war reparations of one hundred thousand tons of pure gold, that's two-hundred-sixty-nine billion *thalers*. That's what the Mazar banksters who designed the *Diktat* want from us."

"Our country will never be able to pay that. For over ten years we have paid, but the debt looms large as ever above us."

"Meanwhile, our children are forced to eat dogs and cats to supplement the watery gruel they get at home."

"Enough is enough. There is a way out for our fatherland and one man can show us the way."

"Who is that?"

"Come with me this Thursday evening to the local beer hall. He will be there."

"What's his name?"

"Albrecht Hayder."

"A politician?"

"Yes, but not like the others. This one is sincere. He wrote a book years ago when the social democrats put him in prison. I will lend it to you. I have a copy autographed by him that I treasure.

"In all these years, Hayder has not said anything different from what he wrote. Most politicians will change their tune based on which way the popular winds are blowing. Not him. He is the real thing and he loves our fatherland. He will save our country."

"A book you say? What is it called?"

"*Meine Herausforderung — My Challenge*."

"Well, we are all facing a challenge," the crippled man replied. "Every one of us, and the next generation even more so."

"We at least knew better days before the war," said the one-eyed man. He pointed to the children. "Those young ones have not. If ever they are going to know better times, we must vote for Albrecht Hayder and his Theudian Socialist party, the *TeSo*"

Hans flipped over his frayed coat lapel to reveal a button with a black crusader cross against a red background. He handed the one-legged man a similar button. "Start wearing it," he said. "Hidden under your lapel for now, so as not to provoke the *Reds*, the Mordechists, who are so numerous in this neighborhood. But soon, the *TeSos* will be in power, the *Reds* will be smashed, and you will be able then to wear the button openly and proudly."

"If they are fighting the *Reds*, why is their flag also red?"

"Because they are also for social solidarity and red is the color of social solidarity. But unlike the *Reds*, the *TeSos* are patriots. They are for Theudaland and our Yeshuan religion. They are not atheistic and 'cosmopolitan' like the Reds, who are in hock to the Socialist International, an organization whose strings are pulled by Mazar banksters."

"I'll be at the beer hall with you on Thursday."

▲ ▲ ▲

The beer hall in the artists' district of Mönchenstadt was packed to the brim. The speaker all were waiting for, Albrecht Hayder, arrived dressed in a neatly-pressed blue woolen suit, with an armband bearing the black *TeSo* cross on a red background. He raised his hand to stop the cheering and took the floor:

"Fellow Theudians, my fellow Eiryans, remember that in life one is either the hammer or the anvil. Our purpose in the Theudian Socialist Workers' Party is to prepare the Theudian people once again for the role of the hammer of Thor. The Verchamps *Diktat* made us the anvil. From now on, we shall be the hammer of Thor. Let other people now, instead of the Theudians, be the anvil."

The crowd applauded him with cries of "Thor's hammer!" and "Heil Hayder."

"If our party is victorious in the polls," continued Hayder, "we will restore to full strength the Theudian armed forces, which are forbidden us by the dastardly Verchamps *Diktat*, that travesty of a peace treaty. And we shall recover all the lands where Theudian people live that were seized from us under the treaty. Only traitors to Theudaland would shy away from flouting the Verchamps *Diktat*, for we have never recognized this cowardly document of revenge as a legitimate treaty. It was imposed on us and we were forced to sign at sword-point.

"Recall that if a people wish to survive, then they are forced to fight others. The struggle for survival means preventing others from stealing your livelihoods. As long as there are people on this earth, nations will rise against nations. Nations, too, need to protect their vital rights, just as an individual does.

"Therefore, we, the Theudian people, will increase the size of our armed forces, as if the Verchamps *Diktat* did not exist, and empower our people. We will smash those who stand in our way. Our rights will be protected only by the point of the Theudian dagger."

There was cheering all around and echoing of phrases from the speech including "Theudian dagger," "Thor's hammer," and "Down with the Verchamps *Diktat*!" Others cried, "Heil Hayder!" and gave the stiff-arm salute. Many had unfurled banners and flags of the Theudian Socialist Workers' Party, the *TeSo*.

Again, Hayder raised his palm to stop the cheering and continued:

"Now, I shall talk of the archfiend of the Theudian people: the Mazar. Let me first describe this creature to you. The Mazar fiend is the greatest of all nationalists. Except that his nation is nothing other than his tribe, which he refers to as 'the chosen people.'

"By lying, the Mazar pretends that he is a Theudian, a Gallian, a Prydenian, and so on. In reality, a Mazar can never be a Theudian or any other national, because if he wanted to be, he would have to give up the Mazar tribe, something he would never do. While aggrandizing his tribe, the Mazar 'denationalizes' other people, depriving them of their national rights, as they have done to us Theudians through the Verchamps *Diktat*, which crafty Mazar bureaucrats drafted right under the noses of the four doddering western heads of government, who themselves knew neither geography nor history.

"The Mazars as a race have great self-regard but lack true culture. True culture springs from the land; and the Mazars have no home, no land of their own, and so they subsist as parasites in the lands of others. The Mazar is a creature that lives off the work of others. Like a termite that eats the wood pillars of a house, the Mazar gorges himself, as he undermines the societies of others.

"The Mazar's real god is gold, not the divinity mentioned in his Good Book. The Mazars believe in no afterlife and thus they seek all their rewards here and now.

"The Mazar is a demon who destroys other people's nations.

The Mazar triumphs with lies but perishes when faced with the truth. Schopenhauer said, 'the Mazar's existence among other peoples is only possible through lies.'

"We must avoid the bastardization of society that arises when the Mazars are allowed to mix with Eiryans. Beware the Mazars, Theudians, don't buy from them or have any kind of truck with them. They do not belong among us Eiryans and must be expelled from our society. Our society must become *Mazarenrein* or free of Mazars."

There was cheering again and cries of *"Mazarenrein! Mazarenrein!"*

"Now, my fellow Theudians, my fellow Eiryans, let me talk to you about Theudian Socialism and how it differs from Mordechism. Theudian Socialism is the highest expression of love for one's fellow humans. Theudian Socialism is learning to do your duty towards one another and society as a whole. Theudian Socialism is interested in the welfare of all the people, not just that of a privileged vanguard of the proletariat, as is Mordechism.

"Theudian Socialism is spiritual, not materialistic, like Mordechism, which is a patchwork of Mazar lies and fabrications. Mordechism is pure deception. Mordechism is materialistic, just as the Mazars are materialistic. Mazars believe in nothing higher than material wealth and Mordechism says any belief beyond materialism is mere 'opium of the masses.' Mordechism promises material goods for its followers but no spiritual goods, as does Theudian Socialism, which preaches pride and joy in helping one's fellow man.

"Mordechism is a perverse tool that serves stock-market manipulating Mazars and global Mazary in their lust for world conquest. Theudian Socialism builds society; Mordechism seeks to destroy it. Remember that Mordechism was the brainchild of a Mazar, a political emigrant from Theudaland to Pryden called Kemuel Mordechai, who cunningly scribbled, usurping our noble Theudian language, the tract, *das Eigentum,* or *Property*, a falsehood commissioned by Mazar bankers to dupe the people of Theudaland and Roxolana.

"The most virulent form of the Mordechist virus is its Roxolan strain, Vozvushnism, which is multiplying fast from an infestation in Eastern Prussau and seeks to infect the Tsar's Roxolana across the border. The vast majority of Bolshevist leaders are Roxolan Mazars, so the movement is in reality, Mazar-Vozvushnism.

"Mazar-Vozvushnism has not taken root in Roxolana and nor will we allow it to spread in Theudaland. We will stamp it out with suitable pesticides in the East where it festers. The best vaccine against the Mordechist virus and its Mazar-Vozvushnik strain is Theudian Socialism. We of the Theudian Socialist Workers Party will destroy the Mordechists and Mazar-Vozvushniks with the great hammer of Thor before they raise their puny mallet and sickle against us."

▲▲▲

Deeply moved by Hayder's speech, the disabled veteran Werner stood in line on crutches for a long while. When he reached the head of the queue, he placed ten *groschen*, one-tenth of a *thaler*, on the table, entered his name and address on the list, signed it duly, and received in return his identity card as member number 234,567 in the Theudian Socialist Workers' party and a loaf of black bread for his family. Werner then hobbled out of the hall with his companion Hans, proudly wearing the *TeSo* button on the outside of his label.

"Should any Mordechist or Mazar-Vozvushnik come up to challenge me with my button," warned Werner, "I shall wield my crutch like Thor's hammer and crush his skull!".

His companion Hans smiled and looked amiably at him through his good eye, "That's the spirit, Werner. The *TeSo* will rule Theudaland soon enough and our children will be able to eat three square meals a day."

▲▲▲

Sunday, 4 June 1933

"What a difference a few months make," said Hans to Werner. "Hayder became chancellor only in February and here we are enjoying an *Eintopf* Sunday, something unheard of in the social-democratic republic or the Kaiser's Empire."

Hans and Werner were sitting on benches at a long wooden table at noon in a beer garden merrily tucking away ample portions of *Eintopf*, the one-pot stew of vegetables and pork that the Theudian Socialist Workers' Party provided party members without any charge on the first Sunday of each month. Along the long table were many of the children from the courtyard of their shared tenement complex. They were all into their second or third helpings of *Eintopf* and there was plenty more of the stew in huge cauldrons on black cast-iron wood-burning stoves in the open air.

Werner said softly to Hans, "At least, the younglings don't have to eat cats and dogs anymore."

They both looked at the children whose clothes were clean and ironed. The boys were all dressed in the brown uniforms of the Hayder Youth, with armbands bearing the black *TeSo* cross in a white circle against a red background. Their troop leader passed by and they all greeted him with a stiff-arm salute and said, "Heil Hayder."

The leader in his early twenties saluted back and said, "Let's liven up the meal, young men, and sing together." He took out a tuning fork, tapped it softly on the table, and then touched his forehead with it. He hummed an 'A' 440hz in his *Heldentenor* voice and then sang solo the introduction to the *Hermann Winkler Lied*, a song once forbidden under the social democratic republic, but which had become commonplace since the Theudian Socialist Workers' Party had won its victory.

In perfect four-part harmony, the children chimed in, as the troop leader had trained them to do. The two veterans sang along, as did those sitting at other tables.

They followed up the song with the national anthem, the *Theudaland Lied*. The impromptu *a capella* concert ended with resounding applause from all the tables and cries of "Heil Hayder" accompanied by the stiff-arm salute. Further cries of "One Leader, One People, One Destiny" and "Hail Victory."

14. PIASTYA

<u>Berstadt, Theudaland</u>
<u>1 September, 1939</u>

Chancellor Albrecht Hayder took the floor before the Theudian parliament:

"For months, we have suffered intolerable torture from one of the outcomes of the Verchamps *Diktat*. Gutanya was and is a historically Theudian city. The name 'Gutanya' means the 'borderland of the Goths.' The Corridor separating western Theudaland from East Prussau, which was imposed by the Verchamps *Diktat* to give Piastya access to the sea, was and remains Theudian.

"Both these territories owe their cultural development exclusively to the Theudian people. As in other Theudian territories of the East, all Theudian minorities living there have been alarmingly ill-treated. Consequently, more than one million people of Theudian blood had in the years 1919 to 1920 to flee their homeland in the East.

"I always proposed peaceful solutions to this intolerable situation, without resorting to pressure tactics, as the West falsely claimed. But all my proposals were rejected — proposals for limiting armaments and even for disarmament, proposals for limiting warfare, and for eliminating certain methods of modern warfare.

"My peaceful proposals for restoring Theudian sovereignty over Theudian territories have all been rejected. So, as we implement these proposals, we do not see ourselves as transgressing any law, because we do not recognize the Verchamps *Diktat* as law.

"We Theudians were forced to sign the *Diktat* under duress — with a gun to our heads — and then this document was considered solemn law. The Western powers are indifferent to the suffering of the Theudian people buckling under the burden of the *Diktat*. The Piastyan statesmen refused all my proposals about Gutanya and the Corridor. Worse, they responded by mobilizing their army and increasing the persecution of our Theudian compatriots under their rule and by slowly strangling the Free City of Gutanya —

economically, politically, and militarily.

For her part, Theudaland has not persecuted the minorities who have come under Theudian rule. No one can claim that any Gallic living in the Saar territory is oppressed, tortured, or deprived of his rights. The Piastyan authorities falsely claim that the Theudians they persecute, including women and children, committed acts of provocation. Let me warn the Piastyans and others that profited from the Verchamps *Diktat* that the Theudaland of to-day is no longer the pliant Theudaland of 1918. No self-respecting power can simply watch the persecution of its people, wherever they may live, and not take action.

"Deputies, if the Theudian Government and its Leader patiently endured such treatment Theudaland would deserve only to disappear from the political stage. But I am wrongly judged if my love of peace and my patience are mistaken for weakness or even cowardice. I, therefore, decided last night and informed the Prydenian Government that I can no longer find any willingness on the part of the Piastyan Government to negotiate seriously with us.

"Meanwhile, Piastyan atrocities are on the rise. Recently, on a single night, there were as many as twenty-one frontier incidents that the Piastyans have perpetrated. Last night for the first time, Piastyan regular soldiers fired on our territory. Since 5.45 A.M. we have been returning the fire, and from now on bombs will be met by bombs. I will continue this struggle, no matter against whom, until the safety of Theudaland and her rights are secured.

"I have resolved, therefore, to respond in kind to the Piastyans. In this regard, I thank the Government of Latium for their constant support of Theudaland, although we will handle this matter ourselves without any foreign help.

"I am only seeking clarity on Theudaland's eastern borders, just as I have declared that the western frontier between Theudaland and Gallia is a final one. I offered Theudaland's friendship and co-operation to Pryden, but my offers were spurned. Theudaland has no designs on the West.

"I have happier news to report on our relationship with Roxolana. Roxolana and Theudaland are governed by two different doctrines. Neither country intends to export its doctrine or invade the other. And so, we have just signed a non-aggression pact with Roxolana, abjuring the use of violence, calling for consultations on certain

European questions, and proposing economic cooperation. Every attempt of the West to sabotage this pact will fail. I will see to it that in the East there is, on the frontier, a peace akin to that on our other frontiers.

"Roxolana and Theudaland did not fight each other in the World War. We will continue that policy. In the last war, Roxolana remained neutral although the Western allies pressured her to enter the war on their side. So, in the capital of Roxolana, this pact was welcomed just as you have acclaimed it.

"For six years, I have built up Theudian defense forces, spending over 90 million *thalers*. They are now the best equipped in Europe. My trust in them is unshakable.

"I ask of no Theudian a greater sacrifice than I am ready to make. There will be no hardships for Theudians to which I will not submit. My whole life henceforth belongs to my people. I am just the first soldier of Theudaland."

Hayder put on an old army coat and resumed, "I have put on again the military coat I once wore proudly in the trenches fighting the Gallics. I will not remove it until victory is secured.

"As a Theudian Socialist and as a Theudian soldier, I face this struggle with a stout heart. My whole life has been nothing but one long struggle for my people, for its restoration, and for Theudaland. There was only one watchword for that struggle: faith in our people. One word I have never learned: surrender.

"I assure all the world that a humiliating November 1918 armistice, as ended the last war, will never be repeated in Theudian history. Just as I am ready at any time to stake my life — anyone can take it for my people and Theudaland — so I ask the same of all others.

"I would like to close with the declaration that I once made when I began the struggle for power in Theudaland: 'If our will is so strong that no hardship and suffering can subdue it, then our will and our Theudian might shall prevail.'"

There was applause all around.

15. FEEDING THE WAR BEAST

Edom Court, Lynden
September 1939

"Now that we are all here," said the Second Lord Edom, "let us begin, as before with a briefing from the minister of war, and we can go over the expected armaments expenditures. The greatest profits from our perspective will be in munitions, so let's start with them. Tell me, war minister. Then we will hear from the house of von Klopp. Kindly report your estimates in North Vespucian *talents*, converting your national currencies so that we have a common basis for comparison."

"For Pryden, *milord*, our expenditures so far on munitions between 1935 and this year, 1939, will total, using an exchange rate of 5 North Vespucian *talents* to one Prydenian *libra*, a mere 500 million *talents*.

"Now having declared war on Theudaland and, following our secret game plan, that should quintuple to 3.5 billion *talents* in 1940, then 6.5 billion *talents* in 1941, 11.5 billion *talents* in 1942, and the same in 1943. If the war lasts longer, well, we'll project again, but I think that is it for now."

"Good, just for Pryden," replied Lord Edom, "that gives us over 40 billion *talents* in munitions purchased, or about 8 billion *libras*, even if stockpiles are left at the end of the war. Now let's hear from von Klopp."

"With the rearmament under Chancellor Hayder, both secret and overt, the government has purchased over the past five years, 2.4 billion *talents* in munitions. I am using an exchange rate of 2.5 *thalers* to one *talent*. We expect that to nearly triple to 6 billion *talents* in 1940, the same in 1941, and will probably increase to 8.5 billion *talents* in 1942, 13.5 billion *talents* in 1943, and jump further to some 17 billion *talents* in 1944. That makes for a total of over 53 billion *talents* for the next five years. For us in Theudaland, that is nearly 133 billion *thalers*."

"So, the figures are comparable in magnitude for Pryden and Theudaland. The other allies and Axis powers don't interest us, because we don't have shares in their armament factories, but we do wish our counterparts in Europe luck, in Latium, and elsewhere. Many of them buy from us, too, and also license our patents."

"Between Pryden and Theudaland," said the war minister, "that makes over 90 billion *talents* just in munitions in the ten years 1935 up to 1944."

"Yes, a handsome sum," concurred the second Lord Edom. "We will devote similar meetings to other kinds of armaments, particularly small arms, artillery, tanks, and other vehicles."

▲ ▲ ▲

In his study, Lawrence Wilmer, the second Baron Edom, "Wilmer" to his close friends and family, looked up at the oil portrait of his late father, Nissim Edom, the first baron Edom, who had died of complications following surgery just after the signing of the Treaty of Verchamps. Lord Nissim Edom had been a pathfinder, the one who had broken down the barriers to Mazars in government. He had been the first peer not to have sworn the traditional oath of office "by the faith of a Yeshuan."

The younger Edom often wondered to himself in the many tricky situations he faced, "How would Father have resolved this?" He often sensed the response come to him in his father's words, although he believed in no afterlife. He felt that the challenges he faced in this second phase of the Thirty Years war were far thornier than those his father had encountered in the first phase. Yet, he doubted that he could ever be as as cunning and clever as his father who had orchestrated the masterful Verchamps Peace Treaty.

Wilmer found the mantle of Grand Master daunting to bear. Was he then weaker than his father? A gifted geographer, educated at the University of Kewford, Wilmer's passion was the Earth and its physical and natural riches. He strove to combine that love with the wide-ranging financial and political responsibilities he had inherited. His bliss was gazing at his great globe that showed the physical features of the world without any nations. This is how the Edom family viewed the world: as a single nation led, from behind the scenes, by the senior Edom of their generation.

16. THE FREE CITY OF GUTANYA

Free City of Gutanya
September 19, 1939

Facing a cheering crowd of thousands, Chancellor Albrecht Hayder stepped forward onto the massive wooden podium, festooned with *TeSo* flags, that had been constructed for him in the central square of the Free City of Gutanya, a formerly Theudian port town on the North Sea, left autonomous of both Theudaland and Piastya by the Verchamps Treaty, and which had now been occupied by the Theudian army:

"Citizens of Gutanya, valiant Theudian soldiers, I am honored to share this great and moving moment with all of you and to tread this soil for the first time.

"Theudian settlers took possession of this land some eight hundred years ago. You may rest assured — Gutanya will henceforth always remain Theudian.

"Gutanya suffered the same fate as all of Theudaland. The Great War, the most senseless struggle of all time, victimized this city and left no winners, only losers.

"Alas, the warmongers and profiteers cynically ignore the lessons of that slaughter of peoples. As that bloody struggle, into which Theudaland stumbled without any war objective, drew to a close, our people longed for a peace to restore the rule of law within and between countries and eliminate all despair. Such a peace deal, however, was not offered to Theudaland. Instead, an arbitrary peace, cobbled haphazardly together by the victors, was forced upon us through a brutal *Diktat*, backed by the threat of invasion.

"Those who forged this unjust *Diktat* intended to break the Theudian people. Many war-weary Theudians trusted that this *Diktat* would bring peace and end privation. Instead, the *Diktat* brought more suffering. The *Diktat* solved no problems but spawned many new ones.

"The drafters of the *Diktat* trampled on the Theudian nation, who, now, after twenty years, has finally arisen to right the wrongs done to her. The Prydenians ignored the fact that, like it or not, the Theudian people are eighty-two million strong and intend to live together.

"Prydenian politicians may howl that they mistrust the Theudian people and their statesmen. However, we, Theudians, rightly have no confidence in those *Diktat* framers, who maliciously ignored history, politics, economics, and ethnicity, ravaged Europe, tore asunder states, suppressed peoples, and destroyed ancient cultures.

"The Piastyan space and Gutanya also fell victim to the *Diktat*. Over the centuries, and through great sacrifices, Theudaland developed the Piastyan space, including Gutanya. All those territories lumped into Piastya under the *Diktat* owe their economic, social, and cultural development exclusively to Theudian vigor, diligence, and creative work.

"The *Diktat's* drafters lopped off provinces from Theudaland merged them into a new Piastyan state, claiming to unite ethnic Piastyans. However, plebiscites revealed that most people in these provinces, regardless of ethnicity, did not want to join the new Piastyan state. Piastya annexed lands settled for centuries by Theudians.

"These past twenty years, the Piastyans failed to maintain the level of progress achieved by the Theudian settlers. If left to the Piastyans, in another fifty years, the area would have reverted to the backwardness that prevailed prior to Theudian settlement.

"Moreover, historic Piastya was never purely Piastyan but rather a motley amalgam of nationalities, a weakness they shared with the former multi-racial Ostmark-Madjar Empire. Never a democracy, Piastya was ruled by a small, parasitic, and primitive aristocracy, supported by a brutal police and military. The Theudians suffered greatly under cruel and jealous Piastyan overlords. Nonetheless, I strove for a reasonable settlement and a peaceful coexistence with the Piastyans.

"To eliminate political insecurity and ensure peace, I sought final borders for our country in the West, the South, and the East. With the late Piastyan leader, Marshal Pilecki, a man of vision, realistic insight, and great energy, I concluded an agreement for a reasonable, bearable cohabitation between both nations. When the great man passed away, the Piastyans ramped up their persecution of Theudians.

"The West bawls loudly if our country expels a single Piastyan Mazar, who may have immigrated only a few years ago. Yet, the West remains blind and mute to the suffering of the millions of Theudians driven from their centuries-old homes by the implementation of the Verchamps *Diktat*. 'Who cares?' argue the Westerners, 'After all, these are merely Theudians!'

"Despite the *Diktat*, Theudaland remains a great power. A great power cannot passively witness the maltreatment of her people by another, far less developed state. No Western power would have tolerated such a similar persecution of their people.

"Two factors made this state-of-affairs particularly intolerable:

"First, Gutanya, a city of undeniable Theudian character, was both barred from rejoining our country and forced to adopt Piastyan language and culture.

"Second, the *Diktat*-imposed Piastyan Corridor severed East Prussau from Theudaland and hindered the region's traffic and trade with us.

"Nonetheless, last Spring, I proposed reasonable solutions to Piastyan leaders for reconciling the Theudians' wish to reconnect East Prussau to Theudaland with the Piastyans' desire for access to the sea, and for reconciling the Theudian character of the city of Gutanya and its desire to return to Theudaland with the demands of the Piastyans for use of the city's port.

"Gutanya would return to Theudaland. An extraterritorial route would be built to East Prussau — at our expense, naturally. In exchange, Piastya would enjoy full rights to the harbor at Gutanya and be accorded extraterritorial access to it.

"Prompted by Pryden, the Piastyan government rejected my proposal. But millions of Theudians who deemed my offer too generous were pleased it was rejected. In response, Piastya mobilized her troops and committed further acts of terror against Theudians. I invited the Piastyan foreign minister to Berstadt to address these questions. Instead of accepting, he hurried to Lynden.

"From Piastyan newspapers, we learned that Piastya would soon annex East Prussau, although it remained part of Theudaland under the Verchamps *Diktat*. Other papers called for Piastya to swallow up Theudaland's Pomerania region. Still others called for moving the border with Theudaland from the Oder River further west to the

Elbe River and annexing of all the Theudian territory between the two rivers, including our capital Berstadt!

"Piastyans vowed to decimate our army. A Piastyan marshal, now retired, even threatened to hack Theudaland and the Theudian army to pieces.

"Amid this anti-Theudian hysteria, tens of thousands of our people under Piastyan rule were abducted, abused, or murdered. The West abetted these atrocities by deluding Piastyans into believing that Theudaland, weakened by the *Diktat*, would not dare to react.

"A haven for the world's warmongers, Pryden encouraged a small megalomanic state, Piastya, to ignite a war. This *Diktat*-born state became a disposable cat's paw for Pryden. Several Prydenian politicians have admitted publicly that their goal is not to defend Piastya but to fight to overthrow the regime in Theudaland.

"When I spoke to the Theudian people in the Rhineland and by the North Sea, I warned of reckless Prydenian war-touts, like the politicians Mountkirk, Ayden, and Dubb-Cuffer, who claim that war with Theudaland is a necessity. These foolhardy shills for plutocratic war profiteers now dominate the government.

"I declared rightly that Theudaland would never capitulate before the West's threats, blockades, or acts of force, but would respond in kind. For that, these warmongers abused their so-called free press to slander me in speeches and articles. They find it acceptable to tout war and defame legally elected foreign leaders, but cynically object to any rebuttals of their nonsense in the so-called controlled press of authoritarian states. If Mountkirk and his cronies think that by their insults and lies, they can drive a wedge between the Theudian people and me, they are gravely mistaken for the Theudian people and I are inseparable.

"Indeed, I am flattered that some Prydenian politicians like Mountkirk criticize me, for that proves that I am defending the Theudian people's interests. I would not want such war-panderers to praise me, because that might suggest I was their stooge, promoting Prydenian interests rather than those of my people.

"Western propagandists allege that the problem in Theudaland is our regime. The warmongers in Pryden say: 'Oh, we don't like the person in power in Theudaland, so we must wage war for the next three years against them to overthrow their regime. Naturally, we will not wage this war ourselves. No, we will put a proxy such as Piastya up to it in our stead. We will profitably provide the cannons and grenades to our proxies and they will provide the cannon fodder to be killed.'

"Perfidious Prydenians! What if we, like them, had declared: 'We do not like the regime presently ruling Pryden or Gallia; therefore, we will wage war against them now'?

"Absent Pryden's warmongering and deceptive defense guarantee for Piastya, a peaceful solution to the conflict may still have been possible. But as September approached, the situation in Piastya became insufferable.

"Pryden once made the pretense of offering to arrange direct talks between us and Piastya. I was willing and, with my government in Berstadt, I waited for two days, but the Piastyans failed to show up.

"On the evening of August 30, I conveyed to the Prydenian ambassador a new proposal for peaceful coexistence, but received no response from Pryden. Instead, Piastya, encouraged by Pryden, declared a general mobilization, and conducted more acts of terror against our people and even assaults on Theudian territory.

"For years, Theudian delegations from the terrorized areas had pleaded for Theudaland to intervene against the atrocities they were suffering at Piastyan hands because, they said, force was the only language Piastyans understood. I bade them be patient, but patience does not mean weakness or acquiescence. So, at last, on 1 September, Theudaland intervened with force to protect her people from Piastyan oppression.

"Our ally, the President of Latium, proposed to mediate. Gallia agreed to this, and so did I. But Pryden rejected Latium's proposal and confronted us with a deliberately impossible two-hour ultimatum to withdraw all our troops from Piastya.

"The naive Prydenians thought our regime would buckle under their pressure, as did the puppet Theudian regime of November 1918, which they had helped prop up with bribes and loans, while bamboozling the Theudian people with their lies. However, today's Theudaland no longer tolerates Prydenian meddling or ultimatums. In contrast, although Theudians suffered great outrages from little states such as Piastya over the last six years, I never sent any of them an ultimatum.

"Piastya has now chosen war, because Western states such as Pryden have egged her on to wage war, to satisfy their greedy goals in world politics and finance. However, rather than gain great benefits the Western states will suffer great losses.

"Western statesmen spread propaganda that the Theudian army was worthless; its equipment inferior; its troop morale deficient; that a defeatist sentiment prevailed in Theudaland; and that the Theudian people were alienated from their Leader. The Prydenians thus misled the Piastyans into believing that it would be easy to resist our armies and to push us back. Duplicitous Prydenian military advisers informed Piastya's foolhardy military strategy.

"Since then, eighteen days have passed and a biblical saying describes well what has happened: 'Man and steed and wagon, the Lord struck all of them down.'

"As I speak, our troops control the whole of what was once Piastya. Since yesterday afternoon, endless columns of the badly beaten Piastyan army have been marching as prisoners of war.

"Yesterday morning, Piastyan prisoners numbered twenty thousand; last night fifty thousand, and this morning seventy thousand. Whatever remains of this Piastyan army will capitulate within a few days and lay down its arms, or it will be smashed!

"The Piastyan commander-in-chief, who threatened to capture our capital, Berstadt, has now fled east, along with his entire government and will no doubt find sanctuary with his masters in Pryden.

"On land, at sea, and in the air, the Theudian soldier fulfilled his duty admirably! The Theudian infantry has proved masterful and our motorized units with their new weaponry, superb.

"The Piastyan air force has avoided bombing Theudian cities, not out of humanity, but because of a fear of a five- or tenfold retaliation. But I have instructed the Theudian Air Force to conduct raids humanely, only against fighting units. In contrast, the Piastyan commander-in-chief has instructed the civilian population to snipe at the Theudian army.

"Yet, I give the Piastyan soldier his due. He fought courageously and desperately, but under confused officers and a top brass ill advised by Prydenian agents. As a result, some three hundred thousand Piastyan soldiers, two thousand officers, and many generals are now Theudian prisoners of war. The Prydenians hung them out to dry.

"The Theudian army has dealt at lightning speed with the enemy, defeating him in scarcely eighteen days. The Piastya of the Verchamps Treaty no longer exists and will not rise again.

"We Theudians have proved that henceforth we shall vigorously defend our interests. The Prydenians lie that Theudian foreign policy is unrestrained and expansionist, seeking to rule over Europe up to the Ural Mountains. In truth, Theudaland's objectives and interests are limited, but we will defend them with determination.

"We signed, on 25 August, a non-aggression pact with the Roxolans, our next-door neighbors, which belies the misleading Prydenian claim that our regime seeks to conquer Eurasia.

"What Eurasia will look like in the future depends foremost on Theudaland and Roxolana, which both have vital interests in this vast area. By our pact, we have relaxed tensions in the region.

"I did not want war with Pryden or Gallia. My goal was to restore cordial relations and trust with our former enemies from the World War. I renounced any claims to alter our western borders with Gallia and have echoed this message in the Theudian press and radio. Thanks to the close relationship between Latium's President and myself, we have now removed all tensions which once existed between Latium and Theudaland.

"However, rejecting all my sincere and friendly overtures, on 3 September, Pryden and Gallia, after confronting us with the impossible two-hour ultimatum I mentioned earlier, declared war on Theudaland.

"The Theudian people do not want war, yet the Piastyans, incited by their masters, the Prydenians, attacked us. The Piastyan public is slowly realizing there was no need for them to wage this war. Only a small clique of international profiteers craves this war and benefits handsomely from it.

"The Prydenians have further declared that this war shall last three years. I pity the Prydenian and Gallic soldiers, who do not know what they will be fighting for, but know it will be for at least three years. What irresponsibility of these governments to drive men to their deaths for dubious vainglorious goals!

"Prydenians believe themselves invincible because of their naval forces. So, once more, under the cover of deceit and dishonesty, the Prydenians are harming Theudian women and children through a naval blockade against Theudaland. Pryden must choose either to conduct their naval blockade in compliance with international law or not.

"The Prydenian objective in this war is not just the elimination of a regime — it is the elimination of the Theudian people, of Theudian women and children, and, therefore, we shall respond in kind to the enemy, because today's Theudaland is assertive and will never capitulate! We know what capitulation would entail. A war-touting Prydenian parliamentarian, Mr. Prince-Chambers, on behalf of his puppeteers, has threatened Theudaland with a second Verchamps *Diktat*, or worse yet.

"Prydenian politicians publicly call for Theudaland to be torn to pieces, and for large sections of her southern lands to be lopped off, to transfer yet more land to Piastya, and create new weak clients states beholden to Pryden. The Theudian people have heard and will fight back! And in fighting for our national existence, we, Theudians, stand firmly united.

"In contrast, I predict the plutocratic world empires of Pryden and Gallia, based on oppressing and exploiting diverse foreign peoples, will break up as a result of this war, just as the four other empires broke up after the World War. As our Savior said, "whoever lives by the sword, by the sword shall perish."

"Moreover, unlike the Prydenians, we Theudians do not conduct cowardly warfare against women and children. In the Piastya operation, I have issued orders to spare the cities, if possible. If, however, a military column chooses to march across the market square and is attacked by fighter planes, then someone else might become a victim as well.

"We have consistently shown mercy. In towns where no terrorists or snipers offered resistance, not a windowpane was smashed. In a city such as Grakowa, for example, not one bomb fell on the city itself. Only the airport and the train station, purely military objectives, were bombarded. If, however, in other cities, the war involves the civilian population, if it spreads to all street corners and houses, then, of course, we must involve the entire city in the war.

"We have abided by this general rule in the past and wish to do so in the future as well.

"I would like, above all, to thank the Theudian people. These past weeks have proven how united and valiant they are.

"We pray that God Almighty, who has blessed our weapons, might enlighten the other peoples, that He might make them realize how senseless will be this war and this struggle of peoples. May He inspire them to restore a peace that the hapless Piastyans gave up because a bunch of infernal warmongers and profiteers from Pryden drove them into a war they did not choose.

"Now, to conclude on a happier note, after twenty years, Gutanya returns to the great Theudian society. Much has changed in Theudaland since then. The former state of social classes has become the Theudian people's state. Once governed by the interests of a privileged minority, Theudaland has now become a commonwealth of all the Theudian people.

"I had vowed not to journey to Gutanya before this city belonged again to Theudaland. I wished to enter this city as its liberator, as I have now done.

"My dear men and women of Gutanya, please see in me an emissary of Theudaland and of the Theudian people who, through me, embrace and admit you into our eternal community, which never again shall let you go.

"Whatever suffering individual Theudians might have to undergo within the next months or years shall be easier to bear by recalling the inseparable community of our great Theudian people.

"To the unity of all the Theudian tribes and to Greater Theudaland: Hail victory!"

17. NEUTRALITY

Edom Court, Lynden
September 1939

"My boy Hayder is doing well, isn't he, Sword-bearer?" said the second Baron Edom to his protégé, the Prydenian war minister, Lawrence Holm-Benslomow, at a midnight meeting of the Peace Pilgrims' Society. "He delivered nice speeches in Gutanya and then in other Piastyan cities. Where does our government now stand with regard to Theudaland and Piastya?"

"Grand Master," replied the war minister, "since 3 September, thanks to the diligent efforts of Globe-trotter in parliament and in the cabinet, we in Pryden and our allies in Gallia are in a state of war with Theudaland; but we have effected no deployment. The poor Piastyans are quite alone."

Globe-trotter, Foreign Secretary Lord Halgefess, the lead warmonger in the Prydenian government, nodded silently behind his silver-colored mask, as though recalling all his browbeating, arm-twisting, or pure blackmailing of his fellow parliamentarians and cabinet members to obtain the declaration of war, ignoring public opinion which was largely opposed to war.

"That's fine for now," replied Lord Edom. "We have got what we wanted. Hayder will serve as a fine spear point with which to impale Roxolana. Having taken over Piastya, he is now right at the Roxolan border. It's not enough for Pryden and Gallia to declare war." He raised his voice. "They must get cracking!"

"That is a tall order, Grand Master," said the war minister calmly, "because Prime Minister Chandler is not playing along with us. He is dragging his feet. That's one reason why we have no deployment."

"Old Nigel Chandler is a bit timid, isn't he?" said Lord Edom. "But at the next parliamentary elections, we'll arrange for Winifred Mountkirk to replace him as prime minister."

The foreign secretary knitted his eyebrows in surprise and disapproval and said, "Winifred Mountkirk, Grand Master?"

The war minister, too, shook his head with skepticism.

"You gentlemen may not like him," replied Edom, "but I own him, just as my father, the first Baron Edom, owned his father, Lord Mountkirk. Winifred owes me his seat in parliament, among many other things. He gambles, is constantly in debt, and has a liking for underage North African boys. And so, Winifred is very malleable. He will serve us as an obedient wartime premier. Plus, he writes, or, rather, edits his ghost-writing, very well. We'll get him to write, or have ghost-written, a history of the war that will be very kind to us!"

"Poor Chandler. So, you will have him pushed out, Grand Master?" asked the war minister.

"Well, Sword-bearer," replied Lord Edom sounding peeved, "Chandler isn't hawkish enough, is he? That's why I never invited him to sit around this pentagram, as his predecessors such as Ashmore had done. Plus, Chandler seems to get along too well with my boy in Berstadt even after reluctantly agreeing in the cabinet to declare war against him."

"When do we get to meet your boy, as you call him, Grand Master?" asked the war minister.

"You don't, Sword-bearer," retorted Edom curtly. "Not for now, at any rate. We need to keep up appearances in wartime and you are belligerents, never forget it."

"I won't, Grand Master."

"But Hayder's new ambassador in Lynden, von Rittersdorf, will meet with us all in *mufti*, at a reception that the prime minister will give shortly. All of you are invited. The ambassador is very keen to push Hayder's agenda of an alliance with Pryden despite our declaration of war. Deep down, Hayder is a Prydenophile, despite his constant railing against our country in his speeches."

The Peace Pilgrims used the expression '*mufti*,' meaning regular dress clothes without their masks or robes, as short hand to refer to their meetings in public outside their secret society.

"Can that come about, Grand Master?" asked the war minister. "An alliance between Theudaland and Pryden?"

The Grand Master shook his head firmly, showing increasing impatience with the war minister. "We need the dialectic, Sword-bearer. We cannot all be allies, or we would have no dialectic, no conflicts, no wars, and no profits. So, an alliance between Theudaland and Pryden is not in the cards. But let von Rittersdorf and Hayder keep hoping for one.

"Our royal family, too, with their Theudian roots, walks a fine line. They have been very pro-Theudian, but that will change quickly now that we have declared war on Theudaland."

"What's next, Grand Master?" asked the foreign secretary.

"I am meeting with the armaments people again day after tomorrow," replied Edom. Turning to War Minister Holm-Benslomow, he added, "You, Sword-bearer, will be there. I expect it."

"Of course, Grand Master," replied the war minister.

"All of us in *mufti*," instructed Lord Edom. "We could invite von Rittersdorf in mask and robe to the outer circle of the Peace Pilgrims because he is a member of our sister secret society in Europe, the Hammer of Thor Brotherhood, but the time is not right, so in *mufti* it will be at the prime minister's reception."

"In our tailored best," responded the war minister.

Lord Edom scrutinized Lawrence Holm-Benslomow. Edom had proposed his candidature to the prime minister as war minister in 1935, first because Benslomow was a member of Edom's tribe and the banker could count on his unconditional loyalty.

That was a time when Edom was observing the rise of his secret protégé Albrecht Hayder, including the covert Theudian rearmament, and foresaw another profitable war, for which the banker would need the right warmongers in the Prydenian government. The chief war-tout was his protégé Foreign Secretary Lord Halgefess; the next most important one was Benslomow.

The Grand Master thought Benslomow eloquent and affable. Son of a Mazar insurance agent, the fellow possessed the drive and pushiness of a seasoned salesman and shined at public relations. Benslomow had deftly made public the Peace Pilgrims' narrative of falsely accusing Theudaland of starting a war with Piastya, when in fact Pryden had used Piastya as a proxy to provoke Theudaland into an armed intervention. After then presenting the Theudians with an impossible ultimatum, Pryden had unilaterally declared war on Theudaland. The Grand Master smiled, recalling his own cleverness and the blind loyalty of his two acolytes in the cabinet who had engineered the Prydenian war declaration.

Yet, Edom faulted Benslomow for being too egocentric, too outspoken, and too ambitious. The banker reckoned that Benslomow would soon grow too big for his boots and, especially in wartime, would need to be replaced by a cooler quieter head. At that moment, Edom made up his mind that, in the future Winifred Mountkirk cabinet, he would arrange for Holm-Benslomow to be replaced by a malleable, but hawkish, Prydenian from an old family, with four Yeshuan grandparents, lest the war become associated too closely with Edom and his tribe.

▲ ▲ ▲

<u>Imperial Palace, St. Paulusburg</u>
<u>October 5, 1939</u>

"You were right, Pavel Arsenievich. The Gallo-Prydenians have cooked up a nice little war for themselves, using Piastya as a flimsy pretext. There was absolutely no need for Pryden and Gallia to declare war on Theudaland over Piastya and then do nothing, not mobilize, nor send the Piastyans any back-up troops or arms. They set the Piastyans up and then hung them out to dry. It is the height of treachery."

"That's the handiwork of the Cabal, Majesty, of those that pull the Prydenian and Gallic politicians' strings. Piastya was a mere excuse for declaring war, just like Illyria might have been in the last war, but was not thanks to our reviving the Three-Emperors-Alliance. Having lost Illyria as a pretext, they chose the Theudian entry into Lotharia as a reason for declaring war."

"So, just like Lotharia in 1914, Piastya has fallen to the Theudians," said the Tsar, "crushed by a new form of warfare that Hayder calls 'lightning war.' He is moving eastwards for now. What does Hayder's incursion mean for us?"

"At first glance," replied Stolbetsin, "Hayder is bent on correcting the wrongs of the Verchamps treaty, recovering what he calls Theudian living-space, and gathering together the Theudian tribes, but more significantly for us, Majesty, we have lost Piastya as a buffer state between Theudaland and Roxolana. We now are eyeball to eyeball with Hayder on our western frontier."

"Despite our non-aggression pact, does he plan to invade Roxolana?"

Stolbetsin nodded. "I believe that the Cabal, having failed in its many attempts to topple our government using the Vozvushniks, the foreign fighters, and other trouble-makers, has now created, with plausible deniability, this bad boy Hayder.

"For the Cabal, Hayder serves two purposes: First, he spooks the Mazars of Europe into emigrating to Falasteen, helping the Cabal build their future national state for the Mazars. Second, he serves as a cat's paw to attack Roxolana."

"So, he does represent a clear threat to us, the 25 August non-aggression pact notwithstanding."

"That is what I believe, Majesty. We should, as the seventeenth-century Puritan dictator of Pryden said, 'trust in God but keep our power dry.'"

"So, we shall. What do you propose?"

"We need to build credible defenses on our western border with Theudian-occupied Piastya. We need to deter a Theudian invasion. And we should move supplies, stockpiles, and industries to the Asian East, where the Theudians could not capture or damage them. We use the tremendous strategic depth of the eleven time zones of Roxolana. No other country enjoys that privilege."

"As part of the non-aggression pact, Hayder offered to divide Western and Southern Piastya up with us and you advised me against it. But we would have got even more territory than Queen Xenia obtained in Eastern Piastya at the partitions of Piastya in the 18th century."

"Stolen property, Majesty. I think we cannot partake of stolen property. Taking part of Western Piastya would have upset the balance of power in Europe. Someday, Hayder will fall and Western and Southern Piastya will be recreated as a sovereign buffer between West and East, even as Eastern Piastya remains part of Roxolana. That would even be to our advantage. We need a windscreen to shield us from the gusts of the West Wind.

"Once Hayder frightens the accomplished European Mazars into fleeing for Falasteen but fails to conquer Roxolana, the Cabal will not allow him to remain in power. They will engineer an attack on him; and at some point, their proxies will confront us directly, militarily or economically."

"Well, Pryden, along with Gallia, declared war against Theudaland on 3 September, but so far nothing has happened except an aborted incursion by the Gallics on the Western border of

Theudaland, possibly just for show. No mobilization. They simply let their ally Piastya fall."

"Yes, the Cabal behind the Prydenian and Gallic governments still harbors hopes that Hayder will invade Roxolana. They are giving Hayder a free hand for now."

The Tsar raised his eyebrows. "Really?"

"And when they perceive that he will not invade us, they will bring him down, perhaps by bringing North Vespucia into the war again."

"That is going to be a hard sell. The public there is so isolationist. No League of States, no ratification of the Verchamps Treaty, no foreign engagements anymore, no Vespucian boys dying in foreign wars."

"Majesty, the North Vespucians, just like their cousins the Prydenians, excel at false flag operations, deceptions, and provocations. They will cause a provocation somehow, as they did in 1915 when they scuttled the passenger ship *Luciana* and blamed its sinking on non-existent Theudian submarines. Perhaps, this time they will provoke the Rebenese since they are vying with them for control of the Pacific. Perhaps the Vespucians will blockade the Rebenese who are so dependent on imports of oil and other raw materials. Then the Rebenese, who are allies of the Theudians, will be faced with no choice but to go to war with North Vespucia and hey presto, North Vespucia is in the war too! They will need to provoke some kind of visible, outrageous attack by Reben. Remains to be seen what form that attack might take. But it needs to be something big and bloody to move the isolationist public to accept a state of war."

▲ ▲ ▲

Imperial Palace, St. Paulusburg
October 1939

"So, at our last meeting, you recommended, Pavel Arsenievich, a build-up of troops in our Borderland Province to face the threat from Theudian-occupied Piastya? As in 1914, once again?"

"Majesty, it is the same war. It is not a second world war; it is merely the second phase of the new Thirty Years War."

"Indeed?"

"Yes, Majesty, call Roxolana a fortress named deterrence. Hayder must feel the strength of our forces even as he abides by the non-aggression pact we have signed, as we did once for our *Dreikaiserbund* with the then Kaiser and Ostmarkian Emperor, to leave the Theudians free to fight in the West without worrying about an Eastern front, since Roxolana has agreed to stay neutral."

"Yes, then why mobilize?"

"Because we need to deter an invasion. One can never trust someone who secretly is supported by the Mazar bankers as Hayder is, even as he swears at the Mazars."

"The Cabal continues to salivate for Roxolan resources and markets, but in vain so far."

"As I have said all along, the Cabal intends to use Hayder as a vehicle to invade Roxolana to break down the barriers to our markets."

"For that, we deploy over a hundred divisions to the borderland?"

"A credible force, Majesty. To keep Hayder looking west and not seeking to attack us in a new Holzweg Plan."

"Geopolitics never change, do they?"

"So long as geography remains the same, Majesty, geopolitics will follow suit."

18. ENDGAME

Hayder's Bunker, Berstadt, 22 April 1945

"The end is near, my Leader," said Magnus Fuhrmann, Hayder's personal secretary. "In a matter of days, Berstadt will fall. Our defenders' ammunition is running out. Our Greater Theudaland, which once stretched from Gallia to Western Piastya, has been reduced to a few streets around the Chancellery above us. The Allied troops are closing in on us. The North Vespucian flag will soon flutter over the Theudian parliament building, as the supreme commander of the Allied forces in Europe has boasted."

Hayder put down his reading glasses and looked up at Fuhrmann. "The Mazar banksters," he remarked, "tricked the North Vespucians into the war, or else we would have won."

In just a matter of months, thought Fuhrmann, the Leader had aged greatly. His hair was now mostly white and there were deep dark pockets under his eyes from lack of sleep. Gone was the aggressive gleam in his eyes, the possessed look he took on as he held audiences of thousands spellbound.

"The Allied supreme command," continued Fuhrmann, "has informed us confidentially that in exchange for the scientific and technological blueprints and processes that we have offered them, they will provide open skies tomorrow and secret safe passage for you, sir, out of the city. They will conduct no aerial attacks. So, we will be able to fly you out tomorrow morning. But the question is to which destination: Hispania or South Vespucia? Have you decided, sir?"

Ignoring Fuhrmann's question, Hayder looked up dreamily at the framed town plan of the future Berstadt, which he had sketched and his chief architect, Arno Schwerte, had finished. "So, the future Berstadt is not to be?"

"The future Berstadt remains as an ideal in the minds of the Theudian people, my Leader. It is engraved deep in their consciousness, thanks to you and you alone. One day, I am confident that they will build it."

"It is my legacy to them, Fuhrmann. Let Berstadt be the capital of Europe one day, the new Constantinople, and Theudaland once again the dominant power on the continent."

Fuhrmann had a worried look on his face. "But your itinerary, sir. You need to decide. Which destination is it to be? I must quickly make arrangements for whichever place you choose."

"Your proposed itinerary for South Vespucia, Fuhrmann, has too many stops. It is too long, too dangerous, too subject to interception. The flight to Hispania is a safe, direct, and short one and I trust my fellow leader, General Vasco, to give me sanctuary. He owes me because our air force helped him win the Hispanian civil war.

"Then later, when the war ends, I will quietly travel to the Republic of Simartina in South Vespucia and settle on the ranch at the foothills of the Andes that General Garrell, the President of Simartina, has offered me.

"General Garrell maintained strict neutrality throughout the war and supplied both sides with beef and grain through neutral Hispania and our submarines in the South Atlantic with fuel. On my advice, many others of our high command are also headed there. We will eventually have a secret Theudian colony by the Andes foothills. In exchange, General Garrell will get to keep the submarines that will take us there and we will provide him with technical advice."

"That will work well, sir. You have made a wise choice to move to South Vespucia in two stages, first by plane to Hispania and later to South Vespucia, when peace prevails and hostile ships no longer patrol the seas.

"Colonel Enrique Martinez, General Vasco's right-hand man, my counterpart in Hispania, will be there to receive you at the air force base in eastern Hispania and will spirit you straight to the impregnable monastery of Montalba in the mountains high above the city of Hannalona. They have readied a comfortable suite of rooms for you and *Frau* Hayder. You will have all that you need. Then, when the time is right, General Garrell in Simartina will expect you."

"How much will the Allies know? After all, Vasco owes his position to the Prydenians and the North Vespucians; they ferried him across the strait of Gibraltar to begin his reconquest of Hispania from the Mordechists. Without the Prydenians and Vespucians and the Theudian Air Force, he would not have been able to defeat the *Reds* in Hispania during the civil war."

"Your escape will be a state secret, sir. Only the supreme Allied commander, the North Vespucian president, and the head of their intelligence service will know for certain. Their counterparts in Pryden will also know—the prime minister, the king, and the head of intelligence. And then, of course, there is Lord Edom. He will know, too."

"Ah yes, the head of the Cabal, Vincent Edom, the third Baron Edom and nephew of the second baron, the late Wilmer Edom, the man who controls the Allies through his grip on their money supply, among other means. Well, they all wanted to destroy me at one point. They never forgave me for not invading Roxolana, but it would have been insanity to do so. It would have cost me a million Theudian lives and would have been an utter failure, as was Norbert Bonacasa's attempted invasion of Roxolana some one hundred and thirty years ago. Geography does not change, Fuhrmann. The Roxolans have eleven time zones to retreat into. No invader has supply lines that long."

"You chose well, my Leader. Nonetheless, for Vincent Edom blood is thicker than water. That is why you will always be protected."

Hayder wrinkled his brow. "Blood? Protected? Whatever are you talking about, Fuhrmann. What blood?"

"I am talking about Moritz Westheimer, sir."

The Leader frowned. "Who?"

"Your family secret, sir. I am on your side, my Leader."

Hayder's expression relaxed. "You have known all along?"

"Your secret is safe and dies with me, my Leader. I say this only to reassure you about your living discreetly and safely in Hispania and later South Vespucia."

"What a strange man, the younger Edom. He has me deposed with one hand and with the other, he protects me."

"As I said, blood, sir. Our secret police discovered that there was a tacit understanding between the Edoms of Pryden and their cousins in Ostmark, the Westheimers, to protect the offspring of Moritz Westheimer, whether recognized or not, and to guarantee their inheritance."

"In my younger days, I did not care where my nest egg came from, Fuhrmann. I just knew my father had left it to me. My late grandmother had never revealed its origin to anyone. But, thanks to it, I had no material worries. I never had too much, but also never too little."

"Through the Edom Bank branch in Vedunia," explained Fuhrmann, "Moritz Westheimer left a modest investment income to your father, as his child by your grandmother, Maria Elise."

"So, you know the details, or at least some of them."

Hayder smiled as he recalled the time that he had spent with the Westheimers and Edoms in their mansion in Vedunia as a young man, conscious he was a poor, illegitimate relative and resentful of the tremendous contrast in circumstances between the legitimate and out-of-wedlock members of the Edom-Westheimer clan.

Nonetheless, through the Theudian secret society, the Hammer of Thor Brotherhood, the Edoms had groomed Hayder for his future leadership role as Chancellor and paved his way though discreet campaign contributions to the Theudian Socialists, a party which Hayder came to dominate.

With the best tutors and coaches that money could buy, Hayder learned elocution, oratory, body language, Prydenian, Gallic, history, politics, geopolitics, military strategy, propaganda, and psychological operations. The training took place during a gap in his official biography, a mysterious ten-month period in 1912-1913 before the start of the Great War, when unhindered travel, communication, and cooperation between Theudaland and Pryden were still possible. He had visited Edom Court in Lynden and even trained at the Tamistowe military intelligence center in rural Pryden.

Fuhrmann continued with a nod, "The Edoms will protect you from afar, my Leader, so long as you stay under the radar. There will be those who will urge you to revive the *TeSo* movement in another place."

"That I will not do, Fuhrmann. I am at the end of my forces, what with my chronic tremors and other ailments. You know all the medications I take. But this defeat is temporary; the Theudian people will rise again and be the greatest power in Europe."

Fuhrman nodded, then said, "My Leader, as you ordered, we will stage suicides of all of you for the public and the press. Your double, your look-alike cousin from Ostmark, will take your place here as of

23 April. The propaganda minister and I have been coaching him in your speech patterns and mannerisms."

"I expect him to follow strictly the script I have left."

"Yes, sir. On the eve of the fall of Berstadt, we will shoot him in the temple, as you have ordered. The official story for the newspapers and history books will be that you and *Frau* Hayder took your own lives, as did the propaganda minister and his family. The media won't care about me or the support staff. We will escape tomorrow and that can be part of the official narrative.

"We have obtained from the morgue, cadavers similar to your type and to that of *Frau* Hayder and, from a veterinarian, even a Theudian Shepherd carcass similar to your pet, Steffi. We have secured suitable corpses also for the propaganda minister and his family."

"You will, as I ordered, cremate them?"

"*Jawohl*, my Leader, we will make a bonfire upstairs in the Chancellery garden, with a special incendiary chemical that will destroy the bodies beyond recognition, leaving only the charred skeletons, which we will bury. Should the Allies doubt that your cousin's corpse is that of the Leader, we would tell them about the charred skeletons in the garden that they might want dug up and examined."

"And the dental records?"

"At your dentist's office in Berstadt, we have had your records and X-rays and those of the others replaced with falsified records containing images of the teeth of the cadavers so that these might someday be published as proof that all of you did commit suicide."

"I take it that the dentist's office was not bombed?"

"No, since his office happens to be near the North Vespucian-owned factories, which were deliberately spared by the Allied bombers, it remains intact."

"Good! You see now why I had instructed Dr. Plaschke to relocate to that district?"

"You gave him prophetic advice, sir. Dr. Plaschke is fully on board and will certify one day, if required, that those are your dental records and those of the propaganda minister and his family."

"All seems in order then."

"What luggage will you be taking, my Leader?"

"I am a simple man, Fuhrmann. You know me. I don't need

much. I eat a vegetarian diet. I don't drink."

Hayder's black-and-tan Theudian Shepherd, Steffi, whined.

"I don't care about luggage," said Hayder. "I will take very little. My valet will prepare my suitcases and my boxes with papers. My only condition is that Steffi comes with us."

"But of course, my Leader. That's why we have a canine carcass of the same breed as Steffi, which we will burn to simulate her death too."

"So, General Vasco's secretary will receive me at the airport in Hispania?"

"Yes, Colonel Enrique Martinez, who is Vasco's deputy, although he bears the modest title of 'aide-de-camp', will see to all your needs. For any major needs you may have, there are, of course, your numbered bank accounts in Helvetia. The bankers will even travel to Hispania with Helvetian francs in cash, if need be."

Hayder shook his head. "Modest, Fuhrmann, *bescheiden*. Such are my needs. But the *Götterdämmerung* plan must go into effect. It must appear and be recorded that I went down with the ship, that I was consumed by the fires of the twilight of the gods."

"That is how it will appear in the world press and then the history books, my Leader."

▲ ▲ ▲

Imperial Palace, St. Paulusburg,
August 1945

"So, now that the Theudians have been defeated, are we to expect a new Verchamps Treaty, Pavel Arsenievich?" asked the Tsar.

"One may call it that, Majesty, and that this is how the Cabal, and their stooges, the Allies, reportedly refer to it. The Cabal will tally up the spoils of the first and second phases of this Thirty Years War. Symbolically, at the behest of the Cabal, the Allies will hold the peace conference once more in Lutecia next year around this time."

"What will be the stakes at the conference?"

"The three big themes will be redrawing once again Europe's borders, extracting reparations from the losers, and trying the losers for war crimes. The innumerable war crimes of the Allies, such as killing three-quarters of a million residents and refugees by firebombing the city of Drehstadt, will not, of course, be discussed. It will be strictly victors' justice, or rather injustice."

"What about Hayder? Are we to believe he committed suicide along with his wife, propaganda minister, and the minister's family? It is absurd. He could easily have escaped. Why would he have killed himself?"

"I share your doubts, Majesty. Hayder was too clever to simply kill himself. I believe he has staged his suicide and escaped. One clue is that the Allies found in the bunker a dead double of Hayder who had been shot in the temple. But unconvinced that the corpse was that of Hayder, the Allies cross-examined the survivors in the bunker, who confessed to the burned skeletons buried in the garden. These were then dug up and examined forensically, including their dentition."

"Now, the papers claim that Hayder's dentist provided the Chancellor's dental records and that these corresponded perfectly to the dentition of the burned corpse."

"Precisely, Majesty, but it was Hayder's dentist. Who is to say those are indeed the remains and dental records of Albrecht Hayder? The records could have been altered and the dentist could well be lying. The *TeSos* are masters of propaganda. Their propaganda minister originated the phrase, 'repeat a lie often enough and it becomes the truth.' The Allies have a lot to learn from them."

"And learn they will. I hear that the former head of Hayder's secret police now works for the Allies. But I wonder where Hayder might have gone."

"Rumor has it that he fled to a remote part of South Vespucia, along with many of his high command. He had many doubles for security and there is no telling if a double was sent to South Vespucia as a decoy, while the real Hayder remained in Hispania, or vice versa. The 1944 briefcase bomb attack against Hayder failed because it was a double who was killed in his stead."

"Hayder is an old fox. But if he, rather than a double, escaped to South Vespucia, he chose well, for President Garrell maintained neutrality during the war, just as we did, and Garrell's country, Simartina, is a beautiful and safe refuge. Might the Cabal or their proxies, the Allies, send assassins after Hayder?"

"I doubt it, both because they can't be sure if indeed their target is Hayder or a double and also because Hayder has done the Cabal's bidding, at least on three important counts."

"Which are?"

"True, he did not invade Roxolana, but he did force many well-off and qualified European Mazars to emigrate to Falasteen, as the Cabal wanted, and he has reunited western Europe in a new 'Holy Latin Empire' just as Karsten the Great once did. The Allies will now keep Europe unified, but under their control, through a military alliance and a common market. Finally, Hayder has helped the Cabal earn a fortune on armaments and munitions."

"What will the new peace treaty look like?"

"I think it will be less vindictive than the Verchamps Treaty, which was deliberately designed to provoke a resumed war. I think this time around, the Cabal is satisfied with their loot. Instead of squeezing Theudaland dry as last time, they will make North Vespucia transfer resources to strengthen Theudian industries. Theudaland will become the industrial powerhouse of the reconstructed Europe."

"But what will the Theudians have to do for the Cabal in exchange for all this reconstruction money?"

"Theudaland will have to commit in writing to paying reparations to Falasteen, probably in perpetuity, a kind of Mazar tax."

"Reparations to Falasteen? But Falasteen is a mandate state of the Prydenians; it is not a sovereign country."

"But not for long, Majesty. The Cabal will ensure that Mazar emigres declare a sovereign state of Moledet. The Theudian reparations will be based on the number of Mazar victims, who perished all over Europe in Greater Theudaland, a form of blood money."

"Can they truly calculate the number of victims?"

"The Cabal will surely come up with an auspicious figure of several millions from their mystical numerology and then affirm that this is the number of victims."

The Tsar shook his head. "Amazing, their tricks never end!"

"That number will then become sacrosanct and anyone questioning it will be accused of anti-Mazarism, which will be made a crime."

"What will happen to the League of States?"

"Its name will change to the World Union. The new entity will overcome some of the League's weaknesses but continue what has been useful in its work."

"Then, I believe Roxolana should join the World Union, Pavel Arsenievich."

"I agree, Majesty, it's better than just staying neutral."

EPILOGUE

<u>Yalta, Crimean Peninsula, Roxolana</u>
<u>September 1950</u>

"I sometimes wonder, Pavel Arsenievich, how our country's fortunes might have fared had you not been wearing your bullet-proof vest on that fateful September day in 1911 or if the archduke had not been wearing in Saraybas, on 28 June 1914, the similar vest that I had gifted him at your behest."

"Much more bloodshed, Majesty, and a much wider second Thirty Years War. In Roxolana, we may well have lost a third of our population to the war."

"Perhaps the socialist revolutionaries, the Mazar terrorists, backed by the Cabal, might have won."

Stolbetsin nodded. "It would have been a very dark scenario. I have not mentioned this before but in dreams and visions, I have seen the parallel Roxolana that would have emerged."

"Yet, you never shared them with me."

"I did not want to bother your Majesty with them."

"So, what did your visions show?"

"A major entry by Roxolana into the two phases of the Thirty Years War, with an enormous loss of life, famines, and destruction."

"Gruesome."

"And a terror-ridden totalitarian state dominated by the agenda and philosophy of a small group of professional Vozvushnik revolutionaries, puppets dancing to the tune of the Mazar banksters. Many decades of terror."

"Well, we are better off then."

"Yes, with all our problems, we are better off."

"Well, in many ways you and I have exchanged roles, haven't we, Pavel Arsenievich? You are the real ruler of Roxolana and our country is better off for it, I must admit."

"You are the Tsar, Majesty."

"I am a figurehead, like the King of Pryden."

"But those reforms in 1905 and then again in 1912 saved the monarchy by making it fully constitutional."

"And me a figurehead."

"Majesty, you, as our monarch, keep our empire, society, and spirit together."

"God's representative on Earth and all that," said the Tsar, slowly stroking his beard. "Well, I am grateful I have occupied the throne long enough to see the Tsarevich lead a normal life, thanks to medical progress on blood coagulants to treat his hemophilia."

"The Tsarevich seems, Majesty, less than keen to assume the throne; he has said so privately to me, although never openly or to others."

"But he will assume the throne. It is his duty," replied the Tsar. "Perhaps in the coming year, I will abdicate and have him crowned as Tsar. He will be the Tsar for the second half of the twentieth century, the Tsar for the Atomic Age."

"Whatever you decide, Majesty, I will fully support you."

"Perhaps the Tsarevich will have better luck in mending our fences with the West."

"The Western allies never forgave us for our neutrality in the war, Majesty, nor for our non-aggression pact, which enabled Hayder to focus all his forces on the Western Front, causing greater Prydenian and Gallic casualties than if he had also faced Roxolana in the East."

"Well, we followed the advice of the ancient Latins, did we not, Pavel Arsenievich? We achieved peace by preparing for war. We were stronger than any invader and the Theudians knew it. They knew that if they took us on, massive and Eurasian as we are, our geography and climate, in addition to our overwhelming troop numbers, would have destroyed their army."

"We have less of a say in world affairs than might have had a totalitarian expansionist belligerent socialist Roxolana."

"We have enough of a say within our eleven time zones, Pavel Arsenievich. Why do we need colonies? We have vassal provinces at our periphery."

"Indeed, Pryden's empire is falling apart. They are losing all their colonies. First, it was Melucca, which has become a sovereign republic. In a matter of years, all of Prydenian Africa will be set free."

"The Prydenians will recolonize it in different ways."

"Should Roxolana not be a part of that liberation struggle of the colonies so as to counter Pryden, Majesty?"

"Let's stick to our borders, Pavel Arsenievich, and to what is important to Roxolana: monarchy, motherland, and mother church — our orthodox faith. Our national identity and our people are what is most important, not distant plots of land with our flag on them."

"Looking back, Majesty, I shudder to recall how the banksters sought to fool and enslave three peoples: the Mazars, the Theudians, and the Roxolans.

"The first victim was their own Mazar tribe, whom they got Hayder to persecute in Europe to force only the rich and qualified among them to emigrate to Moledet, while the poor and less qualified Mazars were left behind to perish in Europe or to drown on ships that were scuttled along the way to Falasteen.

"Second, on the Theudian people, they imposed Hayder, a strongman who was part-Mazar. Following the show trials at the end of the war, the banksters harnessed the Theudians under a new unjust peace settlement — victors' injustice — to pay heavy reparations in perpetuity to Moledet, a sort of Mazar tax.

"The third people, our Roxolans, the banksters were not able to bamboozle and enslave, because we have put up a long and bloody defense. Their threat to us is still not gone, Majesty. We must be ever vigilant."

"I agree, Pavel Arsenievich. Let's keep the banksters and warmongers at bay and Roxolana will be all right."

"Indeed, with our gold-based currency, our refusal to borrow from them, and our prohibition against foreign non-governmental organizations, missionaries, foreign banks, and the like, the banksters denounce us as autarkical and reactionary."

"They will continue to demonize us. I don't know how to stop that. They paint me as an anachronism but don't do the same to the other European crowned heads from allied nations, because they cater to the Cabal and even marry into it, while I do not."

"If they demonize us, Majesty, it is that we are doing what is good for Roxolana and not for them. Your decision to allow all Roxolan Mazars to emigrate to Moledet was wise. Nearly five million of the five million, four hundred sixty thousand in the country have applied to leave."

"Well, the Mazars were always a nation without a country, but since they now have their own country, it is only fitting that they live there."

"In a matter of years, Majesty, after the emigration of all the applicants, there will only be some four hundred and sixty thousand Mazars left in Roxolana."

"I was not aware of the figures."

"Most of the emigrants will settle in Moledet, but a sizeable number, perhaps as much as a third will then emigrate to the Republic of North Vespucia, which has fifty-one percent of the world's Mazar population, and so, although they will not admit it, is the premier Mazar nation in the world, followed by Moledet. Those Mazars that remain in Roxolana are leading productive lives, contributing usefully to our society."

"And for that, Pavel Arsenievich, those Mazars will always be welcome to live freely and practice their faith in Roxolana. I have nothing against their faith or them as a people. We want productive citizens, not revolutionaries, anarchists, and trouble-makers."

"Indeed, Majesty. It might even be useful to offer some of the productive Mazars visible, but not strategic, positions in government, so the tribe's leaders abroad have one less motive to demonize and isolate our country."

"I will keep that in mind, Pavel Arsenievich."

"Increasingly, the West has succumbed to demonic forces, with their governments in hock to satanic puppeteers and moneymen, while we are strengthening our spiritual roots. We may interact more with the West in the years to come, Majesty, if that is you will, but let's always stay aware of who we are and who they are."

"Let us pray that we will be able to stay our course in Roxolana," said the Tsar, "and to brave the western winds."

"Amen," said Stolbetsin.

The two men crossed themselves.

THE END

Made in the USA
Middletown, DE
06 August 2021